# About The Book

When Bob and Kathy set off for their elopement and honeymoon nearly four decades ago, they were ready for the trip of a lifetime, but life had other plans. What should have been a peaceful getaway became a series of unexpected detours, challenges, and unforgettable moments that neither could have predicted. From missed connections to unpredictable turns and unexpected mishaps along the way, Bob's story captures the reality of love and travel. How things can fall apart, come together, and somehow turn into the moments that define us.

Now, thirty-seven years later, Bob Erck looks back with warmth and honesty, sharing a memoir that celebrates the enduring strength of partnership and the humor found in imperfections. His thoughtful storytelling reminds readers that even when life doesn't go according to plan, the journey itself can still be full of meaning, discovery, and love.

"Lost in Paradise" is a heartfelt account proving that sometimes the greatest adventures begin in the most random ways.

# Lost in Paradise

## A True Story

by: Robert Erck

# Dedication

*Thank you to my wife, Kathy, for her love, help and patience in this long journey.*

# Acknowledgements

*Thank you, to my father-in-law, Jack, for the generous wedding present on which this story is based. May you rest in peace.*

*To my longtime friend, Karen, who gave me her infinite knowledge and time. I can't begin to count the endless hours.*

*And my sister-in-law, Christine, and her daughter, Sarah (the teacher) for their input and advice.*

# Table of Contents

Dedication ................................................................................. i
Acknowledgements .................................................................. ii
Chapter 1 An Unlikely Meeting at an Open House ....................... 1
Chapter 2 The Moments Where Time Stood Still ........................ 8
Chapter 3 High Spirits and Higher Ground ............................... 20
Chapter 4 The Night Adrift ........................................................ 31
Chapter 5 Stranded in Paradise .................................................. 37
Chapter 6 A Wild Ride in Pursuit ............................................... 44
Chapter 7 The Lurking Wilderness ............................................ 49
Chapter 8 Paradise Found, or So We Thought .......................... 56
Chapter 9 Adrift in Paradise ....................................................... 62
Chapter 10 Islands in Time ........................................................ 68
Chapter 11 Crossing the Line ..................................................... 84
Chapter 12 The Separation ......................................................... 98
Chapter 13 Three Days in Waiting ........................................... 111
Chapter 14 A Test of Resilience ............................................... 123
Chapter 15 A Story for the Ages .............................................. 135

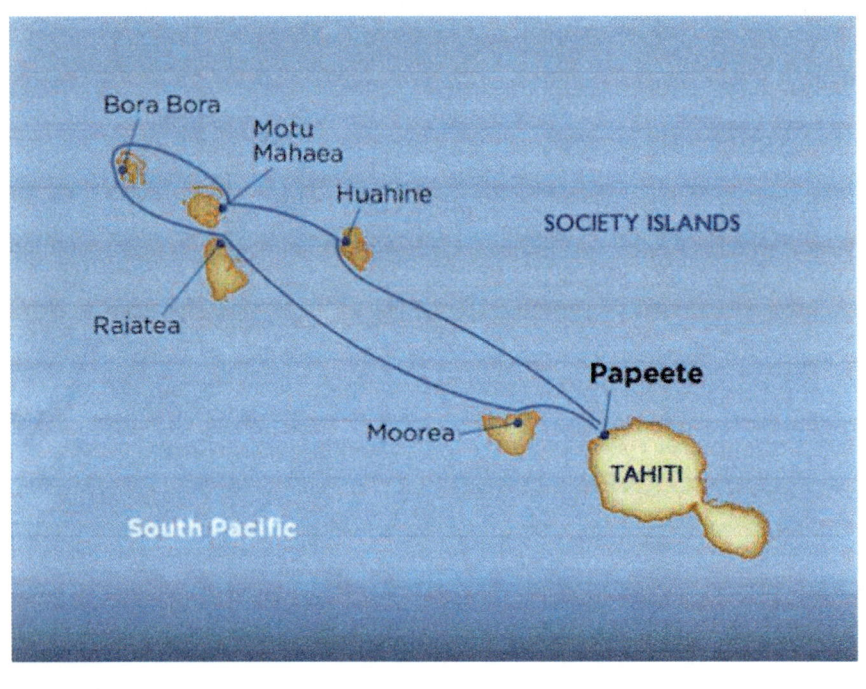

# Chapter 1
# An Unlikely Meeting at an Open House

Another year has gone. Another whirlwind of wins and setbacks, laughter and losses, joy, frustration, and love. And now here we were again—Thanksgiving.

The house buzzed with the kind of chaos only a full family gathering can bring. Children darted between legs like playful puppies. Voices tangled in the air—some telling stories, others yelling over football replays or passing rolls across the table. The aroma of roasted turkey, warm stuffing, and spiced cider drifted through the rooms like a familiar song. It wasn't perfect—but it was home.

Kathy, of course, floated through it all with that quiet kind of grace that made everything feel just a little more magical. She refilled glasses, scooped extra potatoes onto the kids' plates, and smiled in a way that somehow made everyone feel special.

Me? I was exactly where everyone expected me to be—sunk into that old armchair by the fire, a wine glass dangling at the tips of my fingers, plate emptied, loosened belt, ready for the second wave of pie. The firelight flickered across the photos on the mantel—snapshots of a life built one story at a time. But tonight, I knew exactly which story was coming.

It always started the same way.

A clink of silverware against a wine glass.

A hush. And then that one familiar voice pierced through the chaos of a family dinner.

"Tell us the story!"

The room shifted. Chairs turned. Smirks spread. Even the youngest leaned in like they were about to hear a ghost story by candlelight. The wedding. The honeymoon. The cliff. The boat. The brothel.

Yes, that story.

Glancing at Kathy, who already had a look on her face—the *you're really gonna tell it again, aren't you?* She sipped her wine and didn't say a word. She didn't have to. Out of thin air, she handed me the journal.

Leaning forward, I set down my glass and sighed like a man about to dive headfirst into a wild river he'd once swum through blindfolded.

"Some would say," I began, "that our honeymoon was a little... unconventional."

Snorts of laughter echoed around the room.

"You might even say it was a little like that *Tina Turner* song. You know the one—starts out slow and easy... then ends up rough and crazy."

"*Proud Mary!*" someone shouted.

Grinning, I nodded. "That's right. Our journey into marriage? It rolled just like *Proud Mary*."

The laughter came, loud and knowing. As the laughter faded, the room settled again, quiet, waiting for the first line of the story they never got tired of hearing.

So I gave it to them.

The story of how I met Kathy... and how our great adventure into marriage began with an unexpected meeting at an open house in Bedminster, New Jersey.

Kathy, a realtor, was hosting the event at a property owned by the golf pro at Fiddler's Elbow Country Club, who had recently won the New Jersey Lottery. I, a construction business owner, was on the lookout for new projects and decided to attend the open house. Little did I know that this visit would lead me to my future wife.

The early afternoon sun was warming up the quiet suburban streets. The crisp autumn air carried the faint scent of pine and earth, and as I stepped out of my truck, the satisfying crunch of fallen leaves underfoot reminded me of childhood days spent raking leaves in my parents' yard. It was one of those perfect fall mornings when the world felt alive with possibilities, the kind of day when the air was sharp and invigorating, promising new beginnings.

I approached the house with the mindset of a businessman, and my thoughts focused on potential opportunities, returns on investment, and the practicalities of construction. My eyes, trained to assess the structural integrity and aesthetic potential of any property, quickly scanned the building before me. It was a charming colonial-style home with a brick façade and tall windows that invited the sunlight to dance across its panes. Today, it wasn't just the house that would capture my attention—fate had something far more significant in store for me.

As I walked up the path to the front door, the sound of laughter drifting through the open windows broke my train of thought. It was a light, melodic sound that seemed to complement the rustling leaves and the distant call of a passing bird. It was a sound that immediately put me at ease, stirring something deep within me—a sense of familiarity, of home, even though I had never stepped foot in this house before.

The door opened before I had a chance to knock, and there she was. Kathy stood in the doorway with her beautiful auburn hair, her smile as warm as the morning sun, her eyes bright and welcoming. She had an effortless grace about her, the kind that made everyone around her feel comfortable and valued. For a moment, I was caught off guard. I had come here looking for a property, but standing before me was someone who seemed to radiate a warmth that made the entire house feel alive.

Kathy welcomed me with a friendly handshake, her touch soft yet confident. She was dressed in a professional yet stylish outfit that reflected her personality—practical yet vibrant, just like the home she was showcasing. As she led me through the house, her voice was calm and assured, weaving a story about the home's history and its unique features. I tried to focus on her words, but I found myself more captivated by the way she moved, the way her eyes sparkled with enthusiasm, and the gentle cadence of her voice.

Kathy showed me around the property. The house was beautiful, no doubt—a golfer's dream, with views of the pristine greens and a layout that spoke of luxury and comfort. But it was Kathy's presence that made the biggest impression on me. There was something about her that felt familiar, like a melody I had heard before but couldn't quite place. It was as if, in this house on this crisp autumn day, I had found something I didn't even know I was seeking.

Moving from room to room, the conversation flowed naturally. It started with the usual talk of square footage, amenities, and potential renovation ideas, but quickly shifted to more personal anecdotes. We talked about our shared love for the ocean, the simple pleasure of a well-brewed cup of coffee, and our mutual appreciation for hard work and honesty. Each exchange of words built a bridge between us, one that spanned beyond the confines of this house, linking our lives in a way that neither had anticipated.

I left the open house with Kathy's business card in my pocket, but what stayed with me was the feeling that I had just met someone who could change the course of my life.

As I drove away, the crisp air flowing through the open windows of my truck, I couldn't shake the feeling of excitement and curiosity. I had come to Bedminster looking for a project, but I left with something much more valuable—a connection that felt like the beginning of an incredible journey.

Being in the construction business, I saw potential in every building I encountered. I had an innate ability to look beyond the surface, to see the beauty in the raw materials, the possibilities in the blueprints, and the future in the foundation. I approached every project with a sense of excitement and purpose, but when I met Kathy, I found myself feeling something different—something I couldn't quite put into words. It wasn't just about bricks and mortar anymore; it was about the spark of something much more profound.

Our initial meetings were scheduled under the pretense of viewing other properties that Kathy had in her portfolio. Each encounter was an opportunity for me to marvel at her expertise, the way she effortlessly connected with clients, and her genuine interest in helping others find a place they could call home. As much as I admired Kathy's professional skills, what captivated me even more was the way she made me feel, as though I was the only person in the room, like my thoughts and opinions truly mattered.

Each property we toured together was just a backdrop for the growing connection between us. The houses, with their grand staircases and sunlit kitchens, faded into the background as the conversations between Kathy and I deepened. What began as casual small talk about market trends and home values soon evolved into discussions about our dreams, fears, pasts, and our hopes for the future. It was as if, with each new property, we were not just exploring physical spaces but also discovering new corners of each other's souls.

Kathy had a way of bringing out a side of me that I rarely showed to others—a softer, more vulnerable side that I usually kept hidden behind the tough exterior of a construction professional. She made me laugh, and she made me think. She made me want to be a better person, not just for myself but for her. And with each passing day, the realization grew stronger that this was something special, something neither of us could afford to ignore.

Our professional interaction quickly blossomed into something more, a connection that neither of us could ignore. It was as if the walls of formality that had initially surrounded our meetings began to crumble, revealing a space where we could be ourselves—no masks, just two people discovering something extraordinary. The shift from professional to personal was subtle yet undeniable, like the gentle unfolding of a flower in the early morning light.

It was during one of these property visits, as we stood in an empty living room with the late afternoon sun casting long shadows across the hardwood floors, that I felt it—an overwhelming sense of certainty. The room was filled with silence, the kind that feels comfortable and safe, the kind that speaks louder than words. I turned to Kathy, and in that moment, our eyes met in a way that spoke of a deeper understanding. It was as if time stood still, and in that fleeting second, the weight of unspoken words hung in the air between us.

Kathy smiled, a soft, knowing smile that seemed to say, "I feel it too." It was the kind of smile that reaches the eyes, the kind that reveals the heart. I knew then that these meetings were no longer about the properties we were touring but about the connection that had blossomed between us—a connection that was tender yet unbreakable, fragile yet strong.

From that moment on, there was an unspoken agreement between us. We continued to meet under the guise of viewing properties, but there was no longer any need for pretense.

We laughed more freely, shared stories from our pasts that we hadn't told anyone else, and talked about our dreams for the future. Our connection deepened with each passing day, and neither of us wanted to let go. It was a bond that had been forged in the simplest of moments, but it was undeniable, something that had taken root in our hearts and would continue to grow. We both knew, without having to say it out loud, that this was the beginning of something beautiful, something that would shape the course of our lives forever.

# Chapter 2
# The Moments Where Time Stood Still

Our first official date wasn't planned. It was one of those serendipitous moments that life occasionally offers, a decision made on a whim but one that felt perfectly right. After yet another property tour, where the conversation had drifted effortlessly from house specs to shared interests, I found myself hesitating as I walked back to our cars. I wasn't ready for the day to end, and neither was Kathy. So, with a casualness that belied the significance of the moment, I suggested we grab a coffee.

The café we chose was one of those hidden gems tucked away from the bustling streets, a place where time seemed to slow down, allowing its patrons to savor each moment. As we entered, the comforting aroma of roasted coffee beans mixed with the sweet scent of vanilla enveloped us, creating an atmosphere that was both cozy and inviting. The café was small, with warm wooden furnishings and soft, ambient lighting that cast a golden glow over the worn pages of books lining the shelves.

We chose a corner table by the window, where the sunlight filtered through the lace curtains, casting intricate patterns on the tablecloth. The world outside continued its hurried pace, but within the walls of that café, everything seemed to pause, creating a perfect bubble of intimacy for the two of us. We ordered our drinks—I opted for a strong, black coffee, while Kathy chose a delicate latte with a hint of cinnamon—and as we waited, we exchanged smiles.

When our drinks arrived, steaming and fragrant, it felt like the beginning of something more than just a casual conversation.

The clink of the cups on the saucers, the gentle hum of quiet conversation around us, and the soft strains of jazz music playing in the background created a symphony. There was no agenda, no rush, just the two of us basking in the warmth of each other's presence.

As we sipped our coffee, the conversation flowed effortlessly, taking on a life of its own. We spoke of our dreams—Kathy sharing her vision of one day owning her own real estate agency, a place where she could help people find their true homes, and I revealed my desire to build not just houses but places where memories could be made. We talked about our fears—Kathy admitted to her anxiety about taking risks in her career, and I opened up about the pressure I felt to live up to the expectations of those around me.

With each revelation, we peeled back another layer of our personalities, revealing parts we had kept hidden from the world. We spoke of our pasts, the experiences that had shaped us into the people we are today. Kathy shared stories of her childhood, growing up with her sisters, brother, and parents, the strong women who had taught her resilience and kindness. I recounted tales of my early days in construction, the struggles and triumphs that had come with learning the trade from my father's favorite hobby, construction. A man whose hands had been rough with work but whose heart had been full of love.

Each word we exchanged was like a brick laid carefully in place, building a bridge between us—a bridge of trust, understanding, and mutual respect. It was a bridge that grew stronger with every shared moment, a solid foundation for the relationship that was beginning to take shape. There was a magic in those conversations, a sense of discovery that was both thrilling and comforting.

By the time we left the café, the sun had dipped lower in the sky, casting long shadows on the pavement. As we said our goodbyes, there was no need for grand gestures or declarations. The connection we had forged in that small, cozy café was enough and the beginning of something truly special.

We walked away from that first date with a deeper understanding of each other and a newfound certainty that what we had discovered was rare and precious. The bridge we had begun to build that day would carry us forward, supporting us as we navigated the unfolding chapters of our story together.

My connection with Kathy deepened not just through our time together but also through the bonds I formed with her family. The first to welcome me into their lives were Kathy's sisters and her brother. The two women were as strong and nurturing as Kathy herself. The siblings had an unspoken bond, one that came from years of supporting each other through life's ups and downs. When I met them, I knew instantly that these were the people who had helped shape the woman I loved.

The first time I was invited to Kathy's family home, I felt a mix of anticipation and gratitude. It was a modest house filled with memories and the comforting scent of home-cooked meals. The walls were adorned with family photos, each one telling a story of love, laughter, and resilience. Kathy's sisters greeted me with a warmth that immediately put me at ease, their eyes twinkling with the same kindness I saw in Kathy's. Her sisters, with their quick wits and infectious smiles, welcomed me as if I had always been part of their family.

As we sat around the kitchen table, sharing stories and laughter, I felt a deep sense of belonging. It was in these simple, everyday moments that I realized how much Kathy's family meant to her and, by extension, how much they would come to mean to me as well. I saw the way Kathy's eyes lit up when she was around her family, the easy way she laughed with her sisters, and the gentle way she cared for them. It was in these moments that I truly understood the depth of Kathy's love and compassion, and I knew I wanted to be a part of it.

When Kathy's sister mentioned the need for some renovations around the house, I saw it as the perfect opportunity. It wasn't just about lending a hand; it was about embedding myself further into the fabric of Kathy's life, showing her and her family that I was committed to being there, not just for her, but for all of them. The renovations became a labor of love, a project that I poured my heart into, knowing that each improvement I made was more than just a physical change to the house—it was a step towards building a future with Kathy.

Weekends and evenings were spent working on the house, transforming rooms with fresh coats of paint, reinforcing beams, and fixing leaky faucets. Each task, no matter how small, was done with meticulous care, my hands moving with the steady precision of someone who knew that I was crafting something meaningful. Every task wasn't just about the work. It was about the time spent with Kathy, side by side, sharing quiet conversations and laughter as we worked together.

We would often take breaks, sitting on the porch with tall glasses of iced tea, enjoying each other's company. Every stroke of paint, every nail driven into the wood, felt like a promise—a promise of a future where they would continue to build and grow together. The renovations weren't just about fixing up a house; they were about laying the foundation for the life we were creating, one filled with love, laughter, and the steady comfort of knowing that we had each other to rely on.

As the months went by, the house began to change room by room, much like the bond Kathy and I were building. Each repair became more than just a task; it was a quiet act of care, a way of being present and connected. In the rhythm of shared work and the comfort of small moments, laughter over paint, and conversations on the porch, I felt us growing stronger together. The house came to represent something more—a place where love settled into the details and where the foundation of something lasting quietly took shape.

Our relationship blossomed into something truly beautiful, like a garden carefully tended, growing richer and more vibrant with each passing season.

Meeting Kathy's father, Jack, and his wife, Nora, for the first time was a memorable occasion for all the wrong reasons. It was a Sunday afternoon, the kind of day that should have been filled with warmth and welcome, but instead, there was a palpable tension in the air, as thick and heavy as a summer storm waiting to break.

Knowing how much this first meeting meant to Kathy, I made an effort to clear the anxiety that clouded my mind. She had spoken about her father with a mix of affection and frustration, describing him as a man of few words, someone who preferred to keep his thoughts to himself. Jack was the kind of person who observed more than he spoke; his silence was often mistaken for disapproval, but Kathy assured me that her father's quiet demeanor was just his way.

As we pulled into the driveway of Jack and Nora's home, a modest two-story house with a neatly trimmed lawn and a garden that was clearly well-tended, I took a deep breath, steeling myself for what lay ahead. Kathy squeezed my hand reassuringly, but even she seemed a little on edge.

Nora was the wildcard in the equation— a woman known for her strong opinions and her need to control every situation. Kathy had warned me that Nora could be overbearing, and I tried to prepare myself, but nothing could have fully readied me for what was to come.

From the moment we stepped through the door, the atmosphere was stifling. Jack was there, as Kathy had described him—silent and stoic, his expression unreadable. He greeted me with a firm handshake and a nod, and his eyes didn't reveal much. He took a step back, looked at me again, and started jingling the change in his pocket. It wasn't hostility that I sensed but rather a guardedness, as if Jack was holding back, waiting to see what kind of man I really was.

Nora, on the other hand, was a force of nature. She swept into the room with a ball of energy that demanded attention; her voice was loud and assertive, cutting through the air like a knife. She didn't just greet me; she sized me up, her eyes scanning me from head to toe, her gaze sharp and assessing. It was clear from the outset that she was in control, and she intended to keep it that way.

The initial pleasantries felt forced, as if everyone was going through the motions, trying to maintain a semblance of normalcy while the underlying tension simmered just below the surface. Nora took charge of the conversation, steering it in whatever direction she pleased, often interrupting others and dismissing their opinions with a wave of her hand. Jack remained silent, his eyes occasionally flickering towards Nora, but he said nothing to counter her, letting her dominate the exchange.

Every word I spoke was scrutinized by Nora, making me feel more like I was under a microscope. She questioned me about my work, my intentions with Kathy, and even my views on family matters. Each question was laced with a tone that made it clear she was testing me. I answered as best as I could, trying to remain polite and composed, but I couldn't shake the feeling that no matter what I said, it wouldn't be enough to win Nora's approval.

Kathy, sensing the growing tension, tried to ease the situation, gently redirecting the conversation and attempting to include her father in the dialogue. But Jack remained mostly silent, his presence looming like a shadow, while Nora continued to hold court. It was clear that this dynamic wasn't new—Kathy had likely dealt with this for years, navigating the complexities of her father's silence and his wife's dominance.

As the afternoon wore on, I found myself growing more uncomfortable. The weight of Nora's scrutiny became increasingly oppressive. I tried to find common ground, to connect with Jack in the moments when Nora paused to take a breath, but Jack's responses were brief, almost curt, giving me little to work with. It was like trying to reach out across a vast, empty chasm with no guarantee that my efforts would be reciprocated.

Nora sensed my discomfort and seemed to relish it. Her questions became more pointed, her tone sharper. It was clear that she was testing me, pushing me to see how I would react under pressure. I held my ground, refusing to let her rattle me, but I couldn't ignore the sinking feeling in my stomach—the realization that this first meeting was not going as I had hoped.

Kathy, ever the peacemaker, tried to smooth over the rough edges, her gentle words and calm demeanor a stark contrast to Nora's sharpness. She shot me reassuring glances, her hand occasionally finding mine under the table, a silent message of support. Even Kathy couldn't completely diffuse the tension that hung heavy in the air.

By the time we left, I felt drained, as if I had just run a marathon without moving from my chair. The drive home was quiet, both of us lost in our thoughts, processing the afternoon's events. Kathy eventually broke the silence, apologizing for how the meeting had gone, her voice tinged with a sadness that made my heart ache. I reassured her that it was okay, that I understood the dynamics at play, and that this was just the beginning.

I was sure after my first interaction with Kathy's father and Nora that winning them over would take time, and that it would test me in ways I hadn't anticipated. As I looked over at Kathy, I knew that whatever challenges lay ahead, we would face them together.

Despite the awkwardness of that meeting with Kathy's father and Nora, our relationship continued to grow stronger with each passing day. The tension of that day, rather than creating distance between us, seemed to push us closer together as if we both instinctively knew that our connection was something worth fighting for.

We found solace and joy in the simpler things, the everyday moments that brought us together and reminded us of what truly mattered. One of our greatest sources of happiness was our frequent trips to the shore, where we could escape the pressures of daily life and immerse ourselves in the tranquility of the ocean.

Kathy's Uncle Dave and Aunt Mary owned a quaint beach house, a place that quickly became our sanctuary. It was a modest, weathered home with a wraparound porch and creaky wooden floors that spoke of generations of family gatherings and sun-soaked summers. The house was perched just a short walk from the shoreline, where the endless expanse of ocean stretched out before us, its rhythmic waves providing a constant, soothing backdrop to our time together.

Every time we arrived at the beach house, it was as if a weight was lifted from our shoulders. The salty sea breeze greeted us as we stepped out of the car, carrying with it the promise of lazy days and carefree nights. We would unload our bags, the familiar scent of sunscreen and the distant call of seagulls filling the air, and settle into the comforting routine that had become our own little tradition.

Days down the shore were spent in blissful relaxation. We would spend hours lounging on the beach, our skin warmed and slightly burned by the sun, the cares of the world forgotten in the gentle lull of the ocean. I would often bring a book to read while Kathy, ever the collector of memories, would gather seashells as she strolled on the beach, each one a tiny, perfect reminder of our time together. The walks were the best part, the water washing over our feet, leaving a trail of footprints in the damp sand behind us.

The evenings were equally magical. As the sun dipped below the horizon, painting the sky in hues of red, orange, and pink, we would return to the beach house, the air now cooler, carrying the scent of the sea. We would join Uncle Dave, Aunt Mary, and cousins for dinner, and the meal was often simple but hearty—freshly caught seafood, grilled to perfection, accompanied by salads made with vegetables from the local market. The conversation was light and easy, punctuated by laughter that echoed through the house, mixing with the crashing of the waves in the distance.

After dinner, everyone would gather around the old wooden table in the living room, its surface worn smooth by years of use. A deck of cards would be brought out, and we would spend hours playing games, the room filled with the friendly banter of competition and the shared joy of each win and loss. The clink of glasses as we shared drinks, the soft glow of the lamps casting shadows on the walls, and the sound of the ocean outside created a perfect harmony, a sense of peace that was hard to find elsewhere.

In these moments, Kathy and I were completely at ease with each other. There was no need for words to express what we felt; it was there in the way we looked at each other, in the comfortable silence that often filled the space between us, in the gentle touches and the shared smiles. The world outside might have been complicated and full of challenges, but here, in this little beach house, everything was simple and clear. We were together, and that was all that mattered.

Those trips to the shore were a balm for our souls, a time when we could recharge and reconnect away from the pressures and expectations of everyday life. It was during these carefree days, filled with laughter, love, and the calming presence of the ocean, that we realized just how deep our connection had become. We found in each other not just a partner but a true companion, someone who made life's simple pleasures feel extraordinary.

As we would lay in bed at night, the sound of the waves lulling us to sleep, we knew that these were the moments that would define our relationship. It was these memories, that would carry us through whatever lay ahead, reminding us of the love that had grown so naturally between us, as constant and enduring as the ocean itself.

After a few years of growing together, through shared laughter and quiet moments, we felt an undeniable certainty that it was time to take the plunge and get married. Our love had deepened and matured, blossoming into something so profound that the thought of a future together seemed not just desirable but achievable. But unlike many couples who might dream of a grand wedding, with all the pomp and circumstance, we knew that our love was something far more personal and intimate. We chose to honor that by opting for a private elopement, a decision that felt perfectly suited to the quiet strength of our bond.

The idea of a big, elaborate wedding, with its endless guest lists, ornate decorations, and the weight of expectations, didn't resonate with us. What mattered to us the most was the commitment we were making to each other—the promise to love, honor, and cherish for the rest of our lives. We wanted our wedding to reflect the simplicity and authenticity of our relationship, something that was true to who we were and what we meant to each other.

When Kathy's father won a trip to Tahiti on a ship called 'WindStar,' a small cruise ship with sails, and gifted it to us as a wedding present, it felt like a serendipitous blessing, the perfect culmination of our love story. The timing was impeccable, as if the universe itself was conspiring to give us the wedding we had always dreamed of—one that was not defined by grand gestures but by the quiet, profound beauty of a life shared together.

The decision to elope was easy, and it filled us both with a sense of excitement and adventure. The idea of leaving behind the chaos and labor of a traditional wedding for something more intimate and meaningful felt right. It was just the two of us embarking on a journey that would mark the beginning of the rest of our lives.

# Chapter 3
# High Spirits and Higher Ground

Our journey to Maui began as an epic adventure from New Jersey to California and a trans-Pacific flight to Hawaii that felt both exhilarating and endless. With every mile, anticipation built like a crescendo, and our eagerness to disembark was palpable. As the airplane touched down and we descended the steps, a news-worthy sight unlike any other greeted us on the tarmac. There it was, a plane with its roof peeled back as if it had shed its very skin. It was a sight both surreal and shocking, a strange omen that seemed to whisper, *'Welcome to your extraordinary journey.'*

On Maui, a wave of warmth washed over us—not just from the tropical sun but from the unmistakable spirit of aloha that greeted us. The scent of plumeria filled the air, mingling with the salt of the sea, and a soft breeze carried the gentle hum of distant waves. Before we could gather our bearings, a group of local musicians appeared as if conjured by the island itself. They stood at the edge of the terminal, their voices rising in a harmonious chant that seemed to reach into the very soul of the earth.

A woman adorned in a flowing, bright hibiscus-patterned dress approached with leis in hand. She placed the fragrant garlands around our necks, the delicate flowers cool against our skin. The lei, we knew, was more than a mere ornament—it was a symbol of affection, respect, and the welcoming embrace of the Hawaiian culture. As the musicians played a lilting melody on their ukuleles, their fingers dancing over the strings with effortless grace, the woman explained the significance of each element in her soothing, melodic voice.

"This lei," she said softly, "represents the love and warmth of our island. In Hawaiian tradition, it is a way of welcoming you into our ohana, our family."

Kathy's eyes glistened with tears as she inhaled the sweet scent of the flowers. She turned to me, her expression one of awe and deep gratitude as if the island itself was embracing us both. The moment felt like a benediction, a blessing on our upcoming journey and the life we were about to begin together.

The musicians continued their serenade as we made our way through the terminal, their music a gentle yet persistent reminder that we were no longer in the hurried, harried world we had left behind. Each note seemed to unravel the tension in my shoulders, easing the knots of anxiety that had wound themselves tight during the long flight. Even my racing thoughts began to slow, falling into rhythm with the soothing strum of the ukuleles.

As we walked with great anticipation through the small but bustling airport, it was clear that this was more than just a greeting—it was an initiation into the unique culture of Hawaii. The warm smiles of the airport staff, the rhythmic sway of hula dancers who greeted us at the entrance, and the lingering melody of the music combined to create a moment that was both surreal and grounding. It felt as if the island itself was welcoming us, drawing us into its embrace with open arms.

For Kathy, who had meticulously planned every detail of our wedding, this unexpected welcome was like the universe's way of saying 'thank you' for your efforts. I could see the joy in her eyes, the way her entire being seemed to relax and surrender to the moment. This wasn't just an arrival—it was an initiation into the spirit of aloha, into the heart of the island that would witness our vows and hold the memories of our wedding day.

As we stepped out into the brilliant Hawaiian sunlight, the musicians' final chords echoed in our hearts, a melodic promise of the beauty and adventure that awaited us. Kathy squeezed my hand, and I looked into her eyes, seeing my own excitement reflected there. This was the beginning of something extraordinary—a journey not just to a destination but into a new chapter of our lives, one marked by love, connection, and the enchanting spirit of Maui.

At that moment, the world seemed to conspire to ensure our adventure was anything but ordinary. It was as though the universe, with its boundless creativity, was signaling that our story in Maui would be marked by both wonder and whimsy. The air was thick with the promise of new experiences, and every breath we took felt charged with the excitement of the unknown.

Kathy, with her unparalleled gift for planning and her innate grace, had orchestrated every nuance of our Maui wedding with a masterful touch. Her meticulous nature was evident in every detail she managed with such effortless poise. She had thoughtfully arranged for a charming minister and an exceptionally talented photographer to capture the day's magic. It was as though she had painted a picture-perfect canvas upon which our love story would unfold.

Adding a final flourish to her incredible planning, Kathy secured a reservation for us at one of Maui's most exquisite country clubs. The prospect of dining there was like a cherry on top of an already splendidly crafted day. Her ability to curate such an elegant experience, from the ceremony to the celebration, spoke volumes about her dedication and love.

Meanwhile, as our wedding day drew closer, I found myself in stark contrast to Kathy's composed demeanor. My nerves were on edge, unraveling like a frayed thread. The anticipation of the ceremony, the weight of the moment, and the sheer magnitude of the commitment we were about to make all converged into a whirlwind of anxiety. I could feel the tension knotting in my stomach, each passing moment amplifying my apprehensions.

Kathy's serene and confident presence only highlighted my own frailty, yet it was also a source of great comfort. Her calm was a beacon guiding me through the storm of my own emotions. Even as my mind swirled with a thousand worries, her unwavering resolve was a reminder of the love and dedication that had brought us to this pivotal day. It was her strength and grace that grounded me, even as my nerves threatened to take flight.

In the midst of it all, I marveled at how she had turned what could have been a chaotic day into a beautifully orchestrated celebration. As I prepared to step into our new life together, it was clear that Kathy's brilliance and boundless love would be the steadfast anchor in our shared journey.

Our wedding day arrived, and it unfolded with a perfection that seemed almost dreamlike—exactly what one would hope for in the paradise of Maui. The sky was a flawless canvas of blue, unmarred by clouds, stretching endlessly above us. The gentle breeze, a tender caress, danced through the lush palm trees, whispering promises of the future in a language only the heart could understand. The temperature, a perfectly mild seventy degrees, created a serene and comfortable atmosphere, adding to the day's enchantment.

Our chosen venue was a cliff that seemed to touch the heavens, poised on the edge of the world with the Pacific Ocean stretching endlessly beneath us. This spot, as unconventional as it was breathtaking, offered a panorama that seemed both grand and intimate. The vast expanse of the ocean shimmered under the golden sunlight, casting a spell of tranquility and wonder over everything. The cliffs themselves, with their dramatic drop and sweeping views, created a setting that felt both exhilarating and breathtaking, like something out of a romantic fantasy.

The magnificence of this location was not lost on us; rather, it heightened the emotional commitment of the moment. Standing there, with the endless blue of the ocean as our backdrop and the gentle hum of the breeze, we felt a profound sense of connection to the world around us. The unconventional choice of this dramatic setting mirrored the unique and adventurous spirit of our relationship, adding an extra layer of magic to the ceremony.

Smiling to myself, I understood and appreciated how Kathy's dreaming and planning had brought us to this beautiful time and place.

Realizing Kathy was looking at me, I surprised myself, and I blurted out,

"Kathy, what's on your mind?"

With a beautiful smile, almost a grin, Kathy threw her arms wide and shared:

"This day is perfect, Bob. It is as if the universe itself has conspired to make this day a perfect reflection of our love—bold, beautiful, and infinitely expansive."

Finding myself grappling with a sudden surge of nerves, I didn't know how to respond to Kathy's intimate, heartfelt honesty. Shrinking into myself, I realized it was too late to undo the ill-advised decision to indulge in a few drinks to calm my nerves, but it had possibly clouded my mind. Perhaps the gravity of the situation was simply bringing out my fears, and I was being anxious and afraid. As if Kathy was reading my mind and sensing my fears, she looked into my eyes and looped her arm in mine. With an impish smile, she challenged,

"Come on, Bob, we don't want to be late for our wedding."

Kathy and I began our descent down the narrow, winding path that led to the flat, grassy area where our ceremony was to unfold.

Unexpectedly, the once-steady world around me began to shift in startling ways. The Cliffside, which moments before had seemed solid and unwavering, now took on an unsettling tilt, swaying gently like a ship in the ocean.

During this disorientation, my vision became blurry to the point where I couldn't focus, and before I knew it, I was dealing with an overwhelming sense of vertigo.

Anxiety compounded with dizziness had turned the once stunning panoramic view into a hazy fog. I closed my eyes, hoping to clear the fog away, but instead, my stomach started churning, and I felt like I was going to get sick.

The journey down the path should have been like a romantic fairy tale, but instead, I found myself praying the world would stop spinning around and I would regain my composure.

Instead, I began to perspire heavily and noticed beads of sweat forming on my forehead. At that moment, I understood that the gentle breeze was not providing any relief to my overheated body.

"Water… water, Kathy, I need some water," I panted.

Feeling too sickly to care about being embarrassed, I paused and pleaded with my eyes.

"Kathy. Please, I need water."

Magically, as if it were one more thing Kathy had planned for, an ice-cold bottle of water appeared, and I greedily drank it all.

It must have been the water because I was feeling calmer and less stressed, but I knew I would still have the anxious demons to deal with. Realizing my vision had improved a bit, I could see in the near distance what had to be the wedding ceremony site.

Kathy resumed her smile, displaying it with remarkable grace.

"Bob, are you okay to continue?" she inquired playfully.

This beautiful woman knew me so well and understood that my anxieties were trying to win, but she was committed to achieving our goal.

In answer to her, I tucked her arm in mine and proceeded along the picturesque path.

The scene was idyllic, a perfect blend of nature's splendor and human celebration.

As we arrived at the ceremony site, the minister awaited us with a reassuring presence. He was a gentle-faced man in his mid-fifties, exuding a calm authority that radiated peace. He smiled, which helped ease my nerves.

Looking at Kathy, I thought I was dreaming. She was the epitome of elegance and grace. Her wedding dress shimmered in the sunlight, each movement catching the light and reflecting a radiant glow. She seemed to float effortlessly, her beauty illuminating the surroundings and making the moment even more magical. Her auburn hair perfectly twisted into a bun with flowers tucked, their petals soft and fragrant, a crown of nature's own making that added a touch of ethereal beauty to her already radiant presence.

As the ceremony began, my anxiety soared to new heights. The beauty of the setting did little to soothe my racing heart. I could feel sweat forming on my brow again, and it was as though a veil of panic had once again descended upon me. My vision became a yellow-tinted blur, starting at the perimeter and slowly engulfing my entire view as if I were looking down a long tunnel. Everything around me blended into a swirling blur. The idyllic scene, with its ocean breeze and radiant sunlight, became a distant backdrop to the overwhelming focus of my nerves.

Amid the confusion, the minister's pristine white teeth were the only discernible feature. They stood out prominently against the backdrop of my anxiety, serving as a distinct focal point in an otherwise obscure environment.

The contrast between the minister's calm demeanor and my internal turmoil was striking, highlighting the sheer magnitude of my anxiety.

The ceremony was overwhelming for me. I tried to maintain my composure while staying present in the beautiful moment.

Although surrounded by the beauty of the Pacific Ocean and palm trees, my thoughts felt detached from the scene. Kathy's presence was a constant, providing reassurance. Her calm demeanor and gentle voice helped me focus on the vows we were exchanging.

After the ceremony ended, Kathy took my arm and guided me away from the edge of the cliff. Her touch was steady as she led me to a more stable ground. We moved away from the heights, and my emotions calmed. Her support provided stability in a vulnerable moment, demonstrating the practical care that would continue throughout our journey together.

A funny side note. As we were about to enter the country club for our reception dinner, the minister pulled us aside and mentioned,

"Because of your condition, you could get the marriage annulled."

Kathy, ever the defender of our union, responded with a laugh, "He is here of his own accord. I didn't drag him here kicking and screaming." Her humor and strength were a source of comfort and a reminder of the love that had brought us together.

I arrived at the country club in a slight state of disarray and forgot to pack a jacket in my initial nervous frenzy. But the attentive staff, embodying the spirit of gracious hospitality, swiftly provided me with a perfectly tailored jacket. The small act of kindness felt like a gentle reminder that, despite my severe vertigo during our Cliffside wedding, everything was falling into place.

Later, as we settled into our dinner at the country club, the contrast between the earlier chaos and the evening's tranquility could not have been more striking. The restaurant was an oasis of elegance and sophistication, a world apart from the Cliffside ceremony that had left me so disoriented. Plush, opulent furnishings draped in soft, rich fabrics created an atmosphere of refined luxury. From our table, we had a sweeping view of the very cliff where we had just exchanged vows, now illuminated by the soft glow of the setting sun.

The dinner itself was a feast for the senses. Gourmet dishes, artfully presented, arrived one after another, each bite a culinary delight that eased the lingering traces of my anxiety. The fine wine flowed freely, its smooth, velvety texture offering a comforting contrast to the nerves of the day. As the meal progressed, I found myself gradually unwinding, the warmth and sophistication of the setting slowly dissolving the residual tension from the ceremony.

Kathy and I shared smiles and quiet conversations while enjoying the luxurious ambiance of our surroundings. The country club dinner became a poignant celebration of our new beginning.

As the night began to settle in, I reflected on the day's events with a sense of relief and gratitude. Despite the initial chaos and my own overwhelming anxiety, the day had unfolded beautifully. The picturesque setting of Maui provided a stunning backdrop to our vows, and the elegant dinner at the country club drew the perfect close to our wedding day.

The memory of our wedding would always be tinged with a touch of the surreal—a blend of breathtaking beauty and unexpected challenges. It was a day that would remain etched in our hearts, a testament to the enduring strength of our love amidst the highs and lows of life.

# Chapter 4
# The Night Adrift

The next morning was beautiful. The sun was barely risen over the horizon as Kathy and I wandered down the soft, golden sands of the beach. The gentle lapping of the waves at our feet created a soothing rhythm, a calm contrast to the anxiety of the previous day. The early morning air was cool, almost crisp, carrying the scent of saltwater and the faint hint of tropical flowers. It felt like a fresh start, a chance to shake off the remnants of the previous day's chaos and breathe in the promise of a new day.

We walked in silence, the only sounds being the quiet crash of the waves and the distant calls of seabirds greeting the dawn. Kathy's hand slipped into mine, her touch warm and reassuring. We had been through so much in the past day, yet here we were, still standing, still moving forward. The beach stretched out endlessly before us.

As we walked, lost in our thoughts and the simple beauty of the morning, a figure emerged from the mist ahead. He was young, maybe in his early twenties, with sun-bleached hair and a tan that spoke of countless hours spent under the Hawaiian sun. A surfboard was tucked under his arm, and he moved with the effortless grace of someone who belonged to the ocean.

"Morning!" he called out as he approached, a wide, carefree smile on his face. His voice was light, carrying a hint of the local accent, as though he had been born and raised on these very shores. "Beautiful day for a walk, huh?"

"It really is," I replied, returning his smile. There was something infectious about his energy, a reminder of the carefree spirit that seemed to infuse everything in Maui.

His eyes were bright with curiosity. "You two just got here?"

"Yeah," I said, trying to keep the weariness from my voice. "It's been... an interesting start to our trip."

The surfer laughed, a sound as light as the morning breeze. "That's Maui for you. Always full of surprises."

He shifted his weight slightly, glancing around as though checking for any prying eyes. Then, with a conspiratorial grin, he leaned in closer. "You know," he said in a low, teasing tone, "I've got something that might help you really relax. Some good stuff, straight from the islands."

Taken aback by the sudden offer. I blinked in surprise. For a moment, I wasn't sure how to respond. "Oh, no, we're good," I finally managed, trying to be polite. "Thanks, though."

To my surprise, Kathy didn't share my hesitation. With a playful glint in her eye, she turned to the surfer, her voice light. "Actually, I think I'd like a little. How much?"

The surfer's grin widened, clearly pleased with the unexpected sale. "For you, beautiful lady, just twenty bucks for two joints."

Kathy reached into her bag without hesitation, pulling out a crisp bill and handing it over with a smile. The surfer quickly passed her two neatly rolled joints, nodding his thanks before turning back to the ocean. "Enjoy, you two," he called over his shoulder as he trotted back towards the water.

Still processing what had just happened, I watched him go. When I finally turned back to Kathy, she was tucking the joints into her bag with a satisfied smile.

"You bought pot?" I asked, unable to keep the incredulity out of my voice.

Kathy shrugged, a mischievous twinkle in her eyes. "Why not? We're in Maui, Bob. Might as well embrace the island spirit."

For a moment, I stared at her, then broke into a grin. Of course, Kathy would find a way to bring a little bit of adventure into even the simplest of moments. It was one of the things I loved most about her—her ability to find joy in the unexpected, to turn even the most mundane experiences into something special.

As we continued our walk along the beach, the morning sun began to rise higher in the sky, casting a warm glow over everything. The weight of the previous day's ordeal started to lift, replaced by the easy, carefree feeling that had drawn us to Maui in the first place. There was something about the island that made you want to let go of your worries, live in the moment, and savor every bit of it.

The two of us wandered down the shoreline, the sound of the waves blending with the laughter that occasionally escaped us. Every so often, Kathy would reach into her bag, her fingers brushing the small, innocent-looking joints, and a small smile would play on her lips. We had no intention of lighting them up just yet, but their presence seemed to symbolize something more—a reminder that this trip, despite its rocky start, held endless possibilities.

For now, though, we were content to walk side by side, the ocean stretching out endlessly before us, the future as open and inviting as the Hawaiian horizon.

As we boarded the plane at 6 pm for the six-hour flight from Hawaii to Tahiti, the vibrant energy of Maui felt like a distant memory, already softened by the gentle hum of the aircraft. The romance of the wedding, the joy of being newlyweds—it all felt like a distant dream as the dark expanse of the Pacific loomed beneath us. The transition from the sun-drenched beaches to the enclosed space of the cabin was stark, but we embraced the shift with a sense of quiet anticipation. Kathy and I settled into our seats, the familiar clatter of overhead bins and the murmur of other passengers blending into a soothing, rhythmic backdrop.

The flight attendant's voice, warm and professional, guided us through the usual safety procedures, but my mind was already drifting to the promise of our next destination. The flickering lights of the Hawaiian Islands, receding into the darkening sky, were like a tender farewell. Outside the window, the last vestiges of twilight gave way to a vast, star-speckled expanse, reminding us that our adventure was far from over.

Kathy, ever the optimist, leaned back with a contented sigh, her eyes sparkling with the excitement of what was to come. She pulled out a small travel journal, her fingers tracing the edges of the blank pages as if already envisioning the stories they would hold. I watched her, my heart swelling with affection and admiration. Her ability to find magic in every moment, to see each experience as a new chapter waiting to be written, was one of the reasons I loved her so deeply.

As the plane gained altitude and the gentle hum of the engines became a steady lullaby, I let myself relax into the seat, allowing the comforting rhythm of the flight to ease the lingering fatigue from our whirlwind days. The steady glow of the seat-back screens illuminated the cabin in a soft blue light, casting a tranquil ambiance that contrasted with the vibrant energy of our recent days in Hawaii.

The hours ticked by slowly, each minute drawing us closer to the shores of Tahiti. We talked quietly, our conversation drifting from dreams of island adventures to plans for the days ahead. The prospect of exploring the lush landscapes of French Polynesia, with its turquoise waters and vibrant coral reefs, filled us with a renewed sense of wonder.

Kathy reached into her bag and pulled out a small, weathered map of Tahiti, her eyes lighting up as she traced the routes we planned to explore. Her enthusiasm was infectious, and soon, I found myself caught up in her excitement, eagerly discussing the places we wanted to visit and the experiences we hoped to have.

The plane's cabin lights dimmed, signaling that it was time for rest. I glanced out the window one last time. The vast, dark ocean stretched endlessly below us, a serene expanse that held the promise of new discoveries and the adventures ahead of us. I felt a profound sense of anticipation and contentment. No matter the challenges or surprises that lay in wait, I knew that together, we would embrace each moment and continue to turn our journey into unforgettable experiences.

The flight attendants moved gracefully through the cabin, their soft footsteps and hushed voices adding to the serene atmosphere. As I closed my eyes and let the gentle sway of the plane lull me to sleep, I couldn't help but smile at the thought of the adventures that awaited us in Tahiti.

As we neared the island, the captain turned the cabin lights on, signaling that we were about to land. The view from our window revealed the dimly lit shoreline, the docks, and, unmistakably, a ship gliding away from the harbor. I squinted and blinked continuously to make sure I wasn't hallucinating. It was a sight that filled me with a sudden, gnawing dread. The silhouette of the ship, its outline familiar and disheartening, seemed to taunt us from the inky waters.

"Kathy," I said, my voice laced with disbelief. "That's the WindStar."

She turned to look out the window, her brow furrowing as she peered through the darkness. "It can't be," she whispered, but even as the words left her lips, doubt crept into her voice. "It's supposed to be waiting for us."

# Chapter 5
# Stranded in Paradise

The plane touched down, the wheels chafing the tarmac with a shudder that sent a jolt through my nerves. I clenched my fists, trying to push away the growing sense of panic.

As we got off the plane and moved through the lines of fellow travelers at immigration, the reality of the situation began to settle in. The airport, nearly empty at this hour, seemed to echo with our footsteps. There was no bustling crowd, no welcoming committee to greet us—just the quiet hum of machinery, and the distant murmur of night. Eerily, the sterile, overhead robotic voice announced connecting flights in multiple languages, as if reciting them to no one in particular.

We rushed through the airport with a quickened pace, but it was too late. A quick inquiry at the information desk confirmed our worst fear: The WindStar had indeed left the harbor early. Because of a forecasted storm, the captain had made the decision to depart ahead of schedule, and now, we were stranded on the island with no way to reach our intended destination.

Kathy's expression said it all, and with a mixture of disbelief and sadness, she stared at me. She had worked so hard to plan every detail of our wedding and honeymoon, and now, this turn of events.

"We'll figure something out," I said, trying to sound reassuring, though the knot in my stomach tightened with every passing second.

As we wheeled our luggage, we managed to find a taxi outside the airport, its engine idling as the driver leaned against the hood, smoking a cigarette. The man was gruff, his features hard to make out in the dim light. He didn't speak English, only gesturing to the car as we approached. We tried to communicate our destination, the dock where the WindStar was supposed to be, but he just nodded and muttered something unintelligible before loading our bags into the trunk.

The ride was short, too short, considering the fare he charged us—twenty dollars for a three-minute drive. As we arrived at the abandoned dock, I handed him the money. The taxi had barely stopped before the driver tossed our luggage onto the cold concrete and sped off, leaving only the sound of screeching tires fading into the darkness.

The only sound was the distant lapping of waves against the pier. Our eyes adjusted to the absence of light. It was pitch black, save for the faint glow of a single, distant light that flickered like a lone star in the vast expanse of night. My heart sank as I realized we were truly on our own.

Kathy's hand found mine; her grip was tight as we surveyed our surroundings. "What do we do now?" she asked with teary eyes, her voice trembling.

I tried to think. "Let's head towards that light," I suggested, pointing to the glow in the distance. "Maybe someone there can help us."

We picked up our bags and began to walk, the darkness pressing in on us with each step. The dock, once a place of promise and excitement, now felt like the edge of the world, desolate and foreboding. As we walked, the sound of our footsteps seemed to amplify in the stillness, a reminder of just how alone we were.

As we drew closer to the light, the silhouette of a small building came into view. It wasn't a dock office or a hotel, as we had hoped, but a bar with a shabby neon sign flickering weakly above the entrance. The building itself was run-down, its windows covered with grime, and the faint sound of laughter and music drifted from within.

As we stepped into the bar, the first low grumble of thunder echoed in the distance, a fitting prelude to the uncertain shelter we were about to enter.

"This doesn't feel right," Kathy said, her voice tight with unease as she clung close to me.

"Agreed, but we have little choice. We need to find some way to contact the ship, to figure out what to do next."

The interior was dimly lit, with worn-out wooden chairs placed in disarray, and the air reeked of stale beer and sweat. A handful of patrons were scattered about, their eyes dull and uninterested as they nursed their drinks. In one corner, a man played a melancholy tune on an old piano, the notes hanging heavy in the air.

We made our way to the bar, where a payphone hung on the wall, the receiver worn from years of use. I fumbled for change, feeding the machine as I dialed the number for the WindStar. The line crackled with static; the connection was weak and distant, so I could barely hear the voice on the other end, the words garbled and indistinct.

"What are they saying?" Kathy asked, her eyes wide with worry.

"I'm not sure," I admitted, straining to catch anything that might make sense. Desperately, I turned to the woman behind the bar and asked her to call the WindStar. I handed her my credit card, clinging to the hope that maybe a better line would make a difference. The results didn't change, but remained a static and incoherent call. The cost of the call was exorbitant—$175.00 for a few minutes of frustration.

Kathy's eyes filled with tears, her composure finally breaking. "What are we going to do?" she whispered, her voice trembling.

Before I could answer, a young, uniformed US sailor, who had been sitting in the corner of the bar, overheard our plight and approached us. The familiar sight of a service man in a US uniform lifted my spirits.

"Why don't you stay here for the night?" he suggested, nodding towards the bar. "It's too late to do anything now. Go to the dock in the morning. Maybe you'll figure something out then." It wasn't the answer we wanted, but it was the only option we had. Reluctantly, we agreed to rent a small, dingy room on the $2^{nd}$ floor behind the bar.

A storm had begun shortly after we started up the stairs to the room — not a dramatic downpour, but a slow, stealthily unrest in the air. The wind carried a strange, ominous feeling, and the sky had taken on a bruised hue, like the island itself was warning us.

As we stepped inside the room, the dim light from a single bulb revealed the room's stark reality. The walls with peeling wallpaper had turned into a grimy shade of white that added to the sense of neglect. The room was sparse, with a single bed placed in the center that just about fit the two of us. The creaking frame of the bed was covered with a thin mattress barely capable of offering any comfort. The sheets were rough, the mattress lumpy, and the noise from the bar filtered through the thin walls, making sleep an impossible luxury.

The thin walls offered no sanctuary from the raucous atmosphere below, making the idea of restful sleep a distant fantasy.

Kathy sat down on the edge of the bed, her shoulders slumped in exhaustion. She glanced around with a mixture of disbelief and resignation. "I can't believe this is where we're spending our first night in Tahiti," she said, her voice tinged with both frustration and amusement.

The light went on in my head, and I suddenly realized what kind of establishment we had walked into. A real, honest-to-goodness institution of ill repute, a rundown brothel, a far cry from the romantic retreat we had envisioned.

Joining her, I sat down beside her on the bed. The mattress sagged under my weight, making me lurch. I could feel every lumpy spot as I tried to scoot closer to Kathy. I placed my hand on her back, attempting to offer some reassurance despite the discomfort of our surroundings. "It's not exactly what we planned, but we'll make it through," I said, trying to sound more confident than I felt.

As the minutes ticked by, the bar noise seemed to amplify in the small, claustrophobic space. The occasional thud or raucous laugh buzzed through the walls, underscoring the sense of unease that hung in the air. The room, which we had hoped would provide a brief respite, instead seemed to ridicule our situation.

The walls were stained with old cigarette smoke and regret. The air was thick with the scent of cheap perfume. Outside, footsteps echoed down the hallway, too slow, too deliberate. Laughter drifted through the thin walls, mingled with murmurs that carried an undercurrent of something sinister. We exchanged an uneasy glance. The tension in the air was thick enough to suffocate us. This wasn't a place for travelers; it was something else entirely. We both knew it, but neither dared to say it out loud.

We tried to distract ourselves by discussing our next steps, our plans for the morning, and the ways we might contact the ship or find alternative arrangements. Despite the dire circumstances, Kathy's spirit remained unbroken. She found humor in our predicament, and her ability to laugh, even in the face of adversity, helped ease the tension between us. "Look at the bright side. We'll save time in the morning by not having to dress because I'm keeping my clothes on in this place!" she said, clowning a disgusted face.

Lying on the bed, we tried to find a comfortable position. The sounds of the bar continued their relentless intrusion, but we found solace in each other's presence. Despite the grime and noise, there was a small, persistent flame of hope that our situation would improve.

Outside, the storm had grown bolder. Rain began to fall in erratic bursts, tapping against the cracked window like an impatient guest. Thunder rolled again, louder this time, as if punctuating the surreal absurdity of where we had landed. The wind howled down the alley beside the bar, carrying with it the scent of wet earth and seaweed. In that dirty and decrepit room, wrapped in shadows and echoes, the storm felt less like weather and more like a mirror — turbulent, unwelcome, and refusing to be ignored.

The night dragged on, filled with the sounds of arguing, laughter, and the occasional slam of a door. Kathy and I lay in the narrow bed, our bodies pressed together in a futile attempt to find comfort. Sleep eluded us, the tension of the day leaving us both on edge.

As the hours crept by, I could feel Kathy trembling beside me, her breath hitching as she fought back tears. I wanted to comfort her, to tell her everything would be okay, but the truth was, I wasn't sure how. All I could do was hold her close, offering the only solace I had—my presence.

As we drifted off into a fitful sleep, the clamor from below gradually faded into a dull, distant murmur. The room, though far from ideal, became a temporary haven—a place where we could regroup and prepare for the next chapter of our unexpected journey in Tahiti.

# Chapter 6
# A Wild Ride in Pursuit

The morning sun peeked through the tattered lace curtains of the dilapidated room, casting thin streaks of light across the floor where dust danced lazily in the air.

The events of the previous day flooded back with a rush—our missed ship, the unsettling night spent in this dingy brothel, and the uncertainty that hung like a cloud over us.

Kathy stirred beside me, her hair tousled, framing her face like a halo. She wore an expression of vulnerability that tugged at my heartstrings. The sight of her peacefully sleeping by my side reminded me why I felt so strongly about making this trip memorable.

Reaching out, I brushed a loose strand of hair from her forehead.

"Hey, you," I whispered, my voice rough from sleep. "How did you sleep?"

Her lips curved into a small smile, though her eyes held a trace of worry.

"Like a rock, just kidding."

The bar beneath was alive again with diminished sounds through the paper-thin walls—a mix of laughter and muffled conversations, each one a reminder of our strange predicament. The day outside promised warmth, but the humidity clung to me.

"We need to get to the dock," I said.

"Right," she replied, her voice steadying as she slipped on her sandals.

"Let's not waste any more time. Let's grab our bags and head out."

The sun had already risen as Kathy and I stumbled out of the brothel. The night had offered us little respite, minimal sleep to soothe our weary bodies and minds.

The streets were eerily quiet as we made our way to the dock where the WindStar was supposed to be the day before. The only sound was the echo of the soft thud of our shoes against the uneven pavement, a rhythm that seemed to ironically sync with our racing heartbeats. The air was heavy with the scent of saltwater and something else—something earthy and damp that clung to the cool morning breeze. As we approached the dock, a sense of foreboding settled over me, a feeling that the day ahead would be anything but straightforward.

As we made our way toward the dock, I couldn't shake the feeling of being watched. A few villagers glanced our way, their eyes filled with curiosity or something I couldn't quite place. Kathy noticed too, her hand slipping into mine as we walked.

"It's just a small village," I reassured her, but my heart raced. "They probably don't see many outsiders."

"Or maybe they're wondering why we chose to stay in that place," she replied, a nervous chuckle escaping her lips.

As we approached the dock, the rhythmic sound of waves crashing against the wooden posts filled the air, mingling with the calls of seagulls overhead. The sight of the ocean stretched before us, an endless blue that promised adventure and freedom.

The morning air was thick with the remnants of the previous night's rain, the scent of wet earth mingling with the salty tang of the sea. The dock, usually bustling with activity, was eerily quiet in the early hour. A few fishermen were preparing their boats, their voices low and muted, like they were afraid to disturb the fragile calm that hung over the island.

I approached one of the fishermen, an older man with deep-set eyes and hands roughened by years of work at sea. He looked up as I neared, his expression unclear, but there was a kindness in his eyes that gave me hope.

"Morning," I said, trying to keep the worry out of my voice. "I'm looking for the WindStar. We missed it yesterday, and I was wondering if you could tell us how to catch up with the ship?"

The fisherman nodded slowly as if weighing his words before responding. "Aye, the WindStar left late last night. The captain was in a hurry to beat the storm that was brewing. Your best bet now is to head to the next island, Moorea.[1] The ship will be stopping there for a few hours before it moves on."

My heart sank at the confirmation that the ship had indeed left without us. "How do we get to Moorea?" I asked, glancing around the dock, hoping for a simple answer.

---

[1] (Moh-oh-reh-yah)

The fisherman pointed down the shoreline. "There's a plane that flies out of the airstrip on the far side of the island. It's a rough ride, and you'll be traveling with the locals, but it'll get you where you need to go."

I sighed with relief, at least now we had a clearer direction. Thanking him, I felt a mix of relief and anxiety. Relief that we had a way to catch up with the WindStar, but anxiety about what lay ahead. The island was unfamiliar, and the thought of navigating it to find the airstrip left a lump in my throat. But I knew we had no other choice. We had to move quickly if we wanted to make it in time.

The day had just begun, but already, it was shaping up to be another unknown—one that would test us in ways we hadn't anticipated.

However, there was no time to dwell on that. Kathy, ever the pragmatist, was already moving. She said, "It doesn't hurt to get a second opinion," and began scanning the area for signs of life for someone who might be able to help. She soon caught sight of a figure further down the dock and tapped me vigorously to look. It was an old man who looked like he had been up for hours. He was hunched over, working on a small fishing boat with slow but steady movements. Kathy nudged me, and we made our way over to him, hoping against hope that he might have some information, some clue as to what we should do next. After the night's ordeal, we weren't about to blindly follow the first guy we came across.

"Excuse me," Kathy called out as we approached, her voice cutting through the stillness.

The man looked up, his weathered face breaking into a slight smile as he straightened, wiping his hands on a dirty rag.

"Morning," he greeted us, his voice gruff but not unkind. "What can I do for you?"

"We were supposed to catch a ship here yesterday," Kathy explained, glancing nervously at me before continuing. "The WindStar, but we missed it, and we're not sure what to do now. Do you know where we might find it?"

The man's smile faded slightly as he nodded, his eyes narrowing in thought. "WindStar, huh? She left late last night. Captain decided to set sail early, something about a storm coming in. If you want to catch up with her, you'll need to head to Moorea. That's where she's making her first stop."

Relief washed over me, mixed with a fresh wave of anxiety. At least we knew where the ship was headed, but getting there was another matter entirely. "How do we get to the next island?" I asked.

The man scratched his chin, considering. "There's a plane that leaves from the airstrip on the other side of the island. It's not much—just a sandy strip near the water—but it'll get you where you need to go. You'll have to be quick, though. The plane doesn't wait for anyone, and it's usually full."

Kathy and I exchanged a glance, we thanked the man, and without another word, hurried off in the direction he had pointed. The airstrip was a long walk from the dock. I could feel the weight of our situation pressing down on me, a reminder of just how far off course we had gone. But Kathy, with her determined stride and unwavering focus, kept me moving forward, her resolve a beacon in the early morning.

# Chapter 7
# The Lurking Wilderness

By the time we reached the airstrip, the sun was well above the horizon, casting a golden glow over the sandy stretch of land. The plane was already there, a small, rickety-looking thing with faded paint and a few dents in its fuselage. It didn't look like much, but it was our only option. We approached the group of people waiting to board, a mix of locals with their goats, chickens, and children in tow, all chattering in a language we didn't understand.

The pilot, a grizzled man with a cigarette hanging from his lips, eyed us warily as we approached.

"You here for the flight?" he asked, his voice rough from years of smoke and salt air.

"Yes," I replied, trying to keep the desperation out of my voice. "We need to get to Moorea[2]."

The pilot shrugged, motioning for us to board. "You got the fare?" We handed over what little cash we had left, and he nodded, pocketing the money without a second glance.

"Get on, then. We're leaving soon."

The plane's interior was as rough as its exterior, with tattered seats and windows that rattled with every gust of wind. Kathy and I found our seats near the back, squeezing in among the locals and their cargo. The children stared at us with wide, curious eyes while

---

[2] (Moh-oh-reh-yah)

the adults spoke in hushed tones, casting occasional glances in our direction. I felt out of place, a stranger in a strange land, but there was no turning back now.

The plane taxied down the sandy strip, its engines roared to life, drowning out the chatter around us. I gripped the armrest, feeling the sweat bead on my forehead. As the plane lifted off the ground, the sensation of the rickety old plane was terrifying. Kathy reached over, her hand finding mine, looking for reassurance of safety. Through the window, the ocean stretched endlessly beneath us, its vastness both mesmerizing and terrifying. A mother cooed softly to her baby, the lullaby barely audible over the roar of the engines. An old man clutched prayer beads, whispering a plea under his breath. I swallowed hard as the turbulence hit, jostling us like a toy boat in a storm.

The flight was short, but every minute felt like an eternity. The water below us stretched out in every direction, an endless blue that seemed to blur the line between sea and sky. I tried to focus on the horizon, on the destination that awaited us, but my mind kept drifting back to the ship, to the narrow miss that had set us on this course. What if we didn't make it? What if the WindStar was already gone by the time we arrived?

Those thoughts were pushed aside as the plane began its descent onto the island, coming into view through the scratched and foggy windows. It was smaller than the one we had just left, more remote, with dense jungle covering most of its interior and a small town huddled near the shore. The airstrip was nothing more than a clearing in the trees, and as the plane touched down, I felt the brakes catching, and I was relieved.

We disembarked quickly, our bags clutched in our hands, as we made our way across the sandy ground towards the cluster of buildings that made up the town. The air was thick with humidity, the sun already climbing high in the sky, casting long shadows that danced on the ground beneath the swaying palms. The town was small, its streets lined with modest homes and shops, the buildings painted in faded pastel colors that had long since been bleached by the sun.

As we entered the town, we were greeted by a man who stood out from the locals, his pale skin and European features marking him as a foreigner like us. He was tall, with a wiry frame and a shock of unruly brown hair that fell into his eyes. His clothes were rumpled, and he wore a friendly, almost mischievous smile as he approached us.

"Bonjour," he said, his accent unmistakably French. "You must be the couple looking for the WindStar, yes?"

Surprised by his knowledge, I blinked. "Yes, that's us. How did you know?"

The man chuckled, a low, throaty sound that made me uneasy. "Word travels fast on these islands. I'm Jacques," he introduced himself, extending a hand. I shook it cautiously, noting the strength in his grip. "I know where the WindStar will be making her next stop. I can take you there if you like."

Kathy and I exchanged a glance, uncertainty flashing in our eyes. Something about this man; the ease with which he approached us and the way he seemed to know more than he should, made me wary. We had no other options, no other way to reach the ship that was our only connection to the rest of the world.

"We'd appreciate that," I finally said, forcing a smile. "Thank you."

"Bien sûr," Jacques replied with a grin, his eyes twinkling with amusement. "Come, my VW bus is just over here."

He led us to a beaten-up old Volkswagen bus, its paint peeling and rust creeping up its sides. It was packed with supplies—sacks of rice, crates of vegetables, and various other items that hinted at a life far from the conveniences of modern civilization. As we climbed inside, the van creaked and groaned under our weight, and I couldn't shake the feeling that we were stepping into something we might not easily escape from.

As Jacques guided the battered VW bus onto the main road, the town we had just left quickly faded from view. A thick wall of jungle seemed to close in around us with every passing mile. The bus rattled as it climbed the steep, winding road, the tires slipping slightly on the loose gravel that littered the path. The air inside the bus was stifling, a mix of gasoline fumes and the overpowering scent of damp earth and decaying foliage that seeped in through the cracked windows.

As we rounded a particularly sharp bend, the road suddenly narrowed, leaving barely enough room for the bus to pass without scraping against the dense undergrowth that lined the edges. My grip tightened on the armrest, and I jammed on my imaginary brake, thinking I was in control of the bus. I watched the trees blur by, their twisted branches reaching out like skeletal fingers, scratching at the sides of the bus. The jungle was alive with the sounds of unseen creatures—low, guttural calls that echoed through the trees, mingling with the high-pitched cries of birds hidden in the canopy above.

Jacques, seemingly unfazed by the treacherous road, kept his eyes fixed on the narrow path ahead, his fingers tapping a rhythm on the steering wheel as if he were completely at ease. I couldn't shake the fear gnawing at my gut. The further we traveled, the more isolated we became. The road was now a mere ribbon of dirt winding through the jungle, with no sign of civilization in sight.

After what felt like hours of tense, silent driving, the bus suddenly lurched to a halt. I was thrown forward slightly, catching myself against the front seat as the engine sputtered and died. The abrupt silence almost deafening after the constant rumble of the road. We had arrived in what appeared to be a small, forgotten village—if you could even call it that. A few weathered huts stood haphazardly along the roadside, their walls made of rough-hewn wood and corrugated metal. Makeshift tents pitched nearby to shelter the animals from the weather.

Hens clucked nervously, scattering as the bus door creaked open, and a pair of goats stood tethered to a post, their creepy slit pupils following our movements with disinterest. The smell of manure and wet hay hung heavy in the air, mingling with the sharp scent of smoke from a nearby fire. A group of villagers huddled at the fire, their faces half-hidden in the flickering light. They glanced up as Jacques stepped out of the bus, their expressions unreadable as they exchanged a few words in a language I didn't understand.

Jacques picked up on the confusion written across our faces. "Just picking up some supplies," Jacques said over his shoulder, his voice casual, almost too casual, as he motioned for us to stay put. "Won't be long."

My heart pounded in my chest, each beat a reminder of how vulnerable we were in this strange, secluded place on a desolate island. As Jacques moved toward the villagers, I glanced at Kathy, who sat beside me, her eyes wide with the same apprehension that I felt. The bus's interior suddenly felt claustrophobic, the walls closing in as I watched Jacques exchange a few words with one of the men before they disappeared into a nearby hut.

The minutes ticked by as the villagers cast furtive glances in our direction, their conversations in hushed tones, too low for us to hear. My mind raced with possibilities, each more ominous than the last. What if this was a trap? What if Jacques wasn't the friendly guide he appeared to be? The isolation of the village, the way the villagers watched us from the shadows, the eerie silence that hung over everything—it all felt wrong.

While glancing out the window, my eyes scanned the village for any sign of Jacques, but he was nowhere to be seen. The hut he had entered was now dark and silent as if it had swallowed him whole. The uneasy feeling in my gut twisted into something sharper, a gnawing dread that I couldn't shake. My hand found Kathy's, and I squeezed it tightly, offering what little comfort I could in the growing uncertainty.

Just as the tension became almost unbearable, Jacques reappeared, laden with sacks of supplies. He waved cheerfully as he approached the bus, his smile wide and bright as if nothing was amiss. But the villagers' stares followed him, their expressions scary, and I couldn't shake the feeling that we had narrowly avoided something—something dangerous.

Jacques tossed the supplies into the back of the van and slid into the driver's seat, his demeanor unchanged. "Ready to go?" he asked, turning the key in the ignition. The engine roared back to life, the bus shuddering as it pulled away from the village and back onto the winding road. The town quickly disappeared behind us, replaced by dense foliage and the occasional glimpse of the ocean through the trees. Jacques hummed a tune as he drove, his hands relaxed on the wheel, his eyes fixed on the road ahead. Kathy and I sat in the back, our eyes scanning the surroundings as the van jostled and shook, the rough ride only adding to my growing unease.

We were desperate to relax, but the sense of danger still lingered. The road grew rougher, the turns sharper, and with every mile, the feeling of being trapped in a situation spiraling out of control grew stronger. All we could do was hold on and hope that this wild ride would lead us to the safety of the WindStar, and not deeper into the unknown.

Jacques seemed unfazed, his cheerful demeanor unchanged, but I couldn't shake the feeling that we were heading into something dangerous, something we weren't prepared for. I thought this guy was going to take us on a wild ride or, in the worst-case scenario, lead us to our demise.

Kathy, sensing my tension, reached over and squeezed my hand, trying to give me a sense of composure, but to no avail.

# Chapter 8
# Paradise Found, or So We Thought

After what felt like endless hours of chaos and uncertainty, we finally arrived at Jacques' resort. It was as if we had stepped onto the set of a tropical paradise movie. The air was thick with the scent of saltwater, coconut, and fresh flowers. As we emerged from the old VW bus, the sight before us was almost too perfect to believe—like something that belonged in a travel brochure, not in the real world.

A sprawling Tiki hut bar stood at the heart of the resort, its thatched roof rustling softly in the breeze. Guests lounged around, some sipping brightly colored cocktails with tiny umbrellas, others laughing as they sat on stools carved from driftwood.

Huts dotted the shoreline, each one built with bamboo and palm fronds, nestled comfortably under the shade of towering coconut trees. Then, the most beautiful snapshot of the ocean came into view. Crystal-clear aqua blue, stretching out endlessly as if the ocean itself had decided to put on its best dress for the day.

In the center of it all, a 100-foot dock jutted out from the white sandy beach, slicing into the water with purpose, leading straight into the horizon. The sun was shining brightly, casting everything in a golden light.

"This is... incredible," Kathy whispered, her voice filled with awe.

She had a way of taking in moments like this, absorbing every detail with the quiet reserve of someone who truly appreciated beauty when she saw it.

A smile lit my face. It was hard to believe we were still on the same trip that had started with such chaos. I chuckled while recalling missing our ship, spending a night in that dingy brothel, and our antique plane ride with the chickens and goats. This felt like the island's way of apologizing by painting a picturesque scene right in front of our eyes.

Jacques, who had seemed slightly less mysterious since we arrived, led us through the resort. His wiry frame moved with ease as he waved to various staff and guests, who greeted him with warm smiles. It was clear he knew this place well—maybe even owned it. As much as I tried to relax and enjoy the moment, a nagging feeling sat at the back of my mind. We had been let down before, and part of me couldn't shake the thought that this idyllic scene might come with strings attached.

After we were shown to a hut and given a brief moment to take in the views, we headed out for a meal. Fresh fish, perfectly grilled, with sides of tropical fruits and a cold coconut drink that soothed my parched throat.

We ate in silence, Kathy and I exchanged glances that spoke more than words. We were grateful to have a moment of peace and enjoy a delicious meal without incident.

Three hours later, Jacques approached us, his easygoing smile back in place.

"The boat will be anchored soon," he said, his voice tinged with the same calm confidence that reassured me earlier.

"I'll take you to the dock now. They'll send a dinghy for you from the ship."

We settled into the VW bus with great anticipation, hopeful of locating the WindStar. The ride wound through the jungle, a serpentine path shrouded in dense greenery. Each twist and turn revealed glimpses of the island's wild heart: towering trees draped in vibrant vines, exotic flowers peeking through the foliage like hidden gems. The air thickened with humidity, and a palpable tension was building around us.

After what felt like an eternity, we finally arrived at a small, weathered dock. Jaques graciously helped to unload our luggage and wished us well.

Then, without warning, the skies opened up. A brief rain poured down in heavy sheets, each drop hammering the ground with a relentless force as if the island itself were unleashing its fury. We huddled beneath the flimsy shelter at the dock, the sound of the rain a deafening roar that drowned out everything else. The world around us blurred into a watercolor of greens and grays. Then suddenly, just as it started, it was over.

As we waited at the end of the dock, I heard a soft commotion from behind. Turning around, I saw a group of local children rushing towards us. They were barefoot, deeply tanned, and full of energy. Their laughter filled the air as they swarmed around, curious and excited. Before we could say anything, they were all over us.

My mind flashed back to the snorkeling trip we had taken years ago. The swarming children reminded me of a school of ravenous tropical fish rushing to where we were snorkeling. The charter captain had been throwing fish food to attract them, and they surrounded us, nibbling. Their delicate bodies felt like feathers.

Suddenly, I felt someone grabbing at our bags, and my mind focused back on the swarming children. They continued pulling at our camera and even tugging at Kathy's hand. It was overwhelming, their small hands darting everywhere as if we were the most interesting thing they'd seen all week.

"Hey, easy!" I called out, trying to sound gentle, but the surprise in my voice must have given away my discomfort.

Kathy, ever composed, just laughed and tried to gently fend them off as they playfully fought over who would carry our luggage.

Despite their well-meaning intentions, I was still a bit on edge, but Kathy seemed amused by the local children.

Just as we started to regain some organization over our bags, the unmistakable sound of a motor rumbled through the stillness. A dinghy appeared, cutting through the water, its small frame bouncing slightly with each wave. It was headed straight for the dock. A man at the helm waved cheerfully as he approached.

As the dinghy pulled up to the dock, the local children finally released their grip on our bags and stepped back, wide-eyed and still grinning. They waved enthusiastically as we climbed into the small boat, Kathy settling beside me with a contented sigh.

The children faded into the distance as the dinghy began to pull away from the dock. The sound of the motor mixed with the gentle lapping of the waves immediately de-stressed me, and for the first time in days, I allowed myself to breathe a little easier.

As we rounded a point in the shoreline, the WindStar anchored just offshore came into view. What a sight to behold! Its sails were furled, elegant against the horizon. I could just imagine when she's at full sail, with her magnificent sails… six crisp white sails, taut and full, harnessing the wind like captured clouds against the deep blue. Her four slender masts stood tall and proud, a stark geometry against the sky. The ship's hull, a clean, modern line in white, cut cleanly through the water, and a low hum was the only evidence of her passage. Sunlight glinted off polished chrome and expansive windows, hinting at the refined comfort within. She was a powerful presence, a contemporary sailing yacht that spoke of both adventure and sophisticated travel.

We both stared at the magnificent ship in awe and then at each other with a knowing look that finally we would get to start our journey the way we imagined. Kathy squeezed my hand, and for a moment, neither of us spoke. Finally, we caught up with the ship!

As the crew helped us aboard, we were greeted by some curious passengers asking all sorts of questions about missing our departure. I replied, "We arrived at midnight and saw the ship had already set sail; the ship's schedule was set for a 1 am departure." Their voices held a mix of curiosity and genuine worry.

We gave a brief, exhausted summary—the missed connection, the long night, and the brothel. Their reactions ranged from gasps to laughter, but mostly, they looked stunned.

"You're lucky!" one of them finally said, shaking his head. "The captain decided to push off early due to a threatening storm.

Last night's crossing was brutal. You wouldn't believe how many people were seasick. It was pure havoc."

We exchanged glances, a mixture of relief and humor washing over us. Chuckling softly, I imagined the scene: bodies swaying with the boat, the salty spray mixing with groans of discomfort. It was a stark contrast to the serene ride we were enjoying now, and the laughter felt like a release, a momentary escape from the lingering tension of our travels.

But beneath the surface of our lighthearted chatter about the past storm, a thread of unease still lingered. The ocean, both beautiful and unpredictable, held secrets we had yet to uncover. From the expansive windows, I could see a glimpse of dark clouds gathering on the horizon, hinting that the calmness of the sea might be fleeting. For now, though, we let the laughter carry us forward, embracing the unexpected joys of the moment.

The WindStar rocked gently beneath, and the sun dipped further into the horizon. Kathy let out a soft sigh, content for the first time in days. I inhaled the salty air and enjoyed the glorious sunset, believing that this was the peace we had been searching for.

# Chapter 9
# Adrift in Paradise

The WindStar cut through the crystal-clear waters of the Pacific, leaving a trail of white foam in its wake. The horizon stretched endlessly, where the sky met the sea in an almost seamless blend of blue. We spent six unforgettable days aboard, each one packed with a new adventure that unfolded like chapters in a novel we couldn't put down.

Every morning, the sunlight would filter through our cabin window, gently nudging us awake. The soft creaking of WindStar, the smell of the salty air, and the rhythmic sway of the ocean quickly became familiar and comforting. It was as though the WindStar itself was a character in our story, guiding us on this journey through paradise.

"Kathy, you up for French tonight?" I asked, already knowing the answer but loving the way her eyes lit up at the thought.

She smiled, her face glowing with excitement. "Are you kidding? Of course! How could I pass that up?"

Every evening was a culinary experience. The WindStar's dining area, with its soft ambient lighting and elegantly set tables, transformed into a floating French bistro. The clink of wine glasses filled the air as we toasted to yet another incredible day. The delicate flavors of each course—creamy bisques, tender cuts of meat drizzled with rich sauces, and desserts that melted on our tongues. It felt like we were indulging in Parisian luxury, all while surrounded by the vastness of the Pacific.

"Do you ever stop and wonder how we got here?" Kathy said one night, her voice soft, almost dreamy.

Looking at her across the candlelit table, as her eyes reflected the flickering flame. "All the time," I replied, squeezing her hand.

Each island we stopped at added a new layer to our adventure. We had turned into curious tourists wanting to explore every vendor we came upon. Some days, we wandered through bustling markets, where vendors shouted in rapid French or native Tahitian, their voices rising above the hum of the crowd to catch our attention.

*"Par ici, monsieur, madame! Très bons prix, regardez ça!"* one would call out, waving a colorful sarong in the air.

Another, selling wooden carvings, grinned and called, *"Ia ora na! Eiaha e faarue i teie mea! —Don't leave without this!"*

Their stalls were piled high with vibrant fabrics, hand-carved wooden trinkets, and exotic fruits that burst with flavor. I remember the scent of fresh pineapples, their sweetness lingering in the warm air as we strolled through the streets. Kathy's laughter would fill the space between us whenever I tried my hand at haggling; my broken attempts at the local language only made her giggle more. We were having the time of our lives.

On other days, we found ourselves on beaches that felt untouched by time. The sand beneath our feet was impossibly white, soft as powder, and the water… oh, the water. It shimmered like a thousand diamonds scattered across the surface under the golden sun, inviting us to wade in and lose ourselves in its warmth. We would walk for hours, sometimes in comfortable silence, other times sharing stories, dreams, and plans for the future while basking in the warmth of the sun. It was in those quiet moments that I felt the magnitude of what we were building together, a life filled with moments like these that no one could ever take from us.

"Could you get used to this?" Kathy asked.

"Used to what?" I teased. "The sun, the sand, or my amazing company?"

She nudged me playfully. "All of it. But mostly the company," she said, her voice filled with affection.

But it wasn't all quiet beaches and market shopping. We sought adventure, too. One day, we went snorkeling, and as soon as I plunged into the warm waters, I was awestruck. Beneath the surface was a world that felt surreal. Schools of fish swam past us in synchronized harmony, their vibrant colors flashing in the sunlight. Coral reefs stretched like underwater forests, teeming with life, each creature moving with a grace and purpose that was mesmerizing. I could hear Kathy's delighted squeal through her snorkel as a particularly curious fish swam right up to her, inspecting her as a new visitor in its world.

The adrenaline rush of shark watching and feeding, though, was something else entirely. A group of us boarded three Tahitian long boats and maneuvered to a coral reef with shallow waters and a strong current.

"You nervous?" I asked, my voice laced with amusement.

"A little," Kathy chuckled nervously. "I mean… they're sharks."

I grinned, leaning against the railing. "Relax. They are more interested in the fish than you."

Then, in the strong current, the bobbing boats anchored 20 feet from each other and tethered a rope to each. We got into the turbulent water with snorkels and clung to the tethered rope. The locals would throw small fish into the area, and the sharks came in a boiling frenzy to devour their dinner. The sharks came within 3 feet of us. The guy next to me had the safety rope at his mid-waist with his arms and legs dangling forward towards the sharks. He was crazy. I was frantically pushing and kicking to get away from the frenzy.

\*\*\*

The WindStar glided into Huahine's[3] harbor, its engine a low hum beneath the morning's gentle breeze, like a lullaby that promised the adventures of a new day. The sun was just waking, casting long fingers of gold across the horizon, stretching out over the water in a delicate embrace. Each ray shimmered like liquid gold, reflecting off the tranquil waters of Tahiti, transforming the sea into a dazzling canvas of light.

As the days on WindStar slipped by in a blissful blur of experiences, the end of our time on the water came quicker than I expected.

As the island stood before us, it resembled a painting come to life. Lush green mountains rise dramatically from the deep blue sea, their peaks shrouded in a mystical veil of mist. The air was fragrant with the scent of blooming hibiscus and salt, intoxicating in its freshness. Palm trees lined the shore, their fronds dancing in the

---

[3] (Hoo-wah-hee-neh)

warm breeze, whispering secrets of the island. Colorful fishing boats bobbed lazily in the distance, their hulls splashed with vibrant hues.

Standing at the deck railing, my fingers tracing the smooth wood, I felt the warmth of the sun seep into my skin, a comforting reminder of our new beginning. Beside me, Kathy was lost in thought, her eyes fixed on the horizon as if searching for something.

Upon docking in Huahine, we could feel the energy of the city buzzing with life. The sounds of traffic, the hum of people going about their day, and the distant rhythm of island music were a sharp contrast to the gentle sway of the WindStar. It was like stepping into a different world. We had the most fun while on mopeds, being guided by a local barefoot teenager through the outback. The jungle waterfall was spectacular enough to take our breath away.

Taking sail for Papeete[4], the capital of Tahiti, was especially memorable, as several shipmates were absent at departure time. Kathy excitedly pointed out that the gangplank was being removed. As we peered over the rail, we were shocked to sense WindStar's movement. Our eyes met, and both of us burst out laughing, as we knew how the missing shipmates would feel when they arrived at the dock.

While sailing to Papeete, we must mention the last memorable dinner while on WindStar. We were served the specialty dish of the evening: Fafaru, a traditional Polynesian fish dish. Fafaru is known for its unique and pungent fermented flavor and is surprisingly sweet.

As WindStar docked, the gentle thud against the wooden pier sent a jolt of reality crashing back in, but it only fueled my

---

[4] Pa-peh-EH-teh

determination to embrace every moment. We got off and stepped onto the vibrant streets of Papeete, where life swirled around us like a vivid tapestry.

# Chapter 10
# Islands in Time

The air was charged with life—locals on scooters zipped by, weaving through the narrow roads like colorful fish darting through a coral reef, their engines buzzing like bees, filling the atmosphere with a lively hum. Street vendors called out in rapid French, their voices a symphony of sounds that blended into a chaotic yet beautiful melody. They beckoned us with broad smiles, offering everything from freshly sliced pineapples glistening under the sun to intricately hand-carved trinkets that seemed to whisper tales of the island.

The aroma of grilled fish wafted through the air, mingling with the sweet fragrance of tropical flowers that seemed to bloom everywhere we turned. Vivid colors splashed across every surface—brightly painted buildings, vibrant fabrics fluttering in the breeze, and the deep blue of the sky that seemed to stretch on forever. The rhythm of island life thrummed around us, pulsing with energy that ignited our curiosity.

"Have we stepped into a dream?" she murmured, her eyes wide as she absorbed the sights and sounds, the wonder evident in her voice.

"It seems as though we have," I agreed, glancing down at her, captivated by the way her face lit up with excitement. "It's like the island has its own rhythm."

We wandered through the bustling streets, each step taking us deeper into the island's vibrant pulse. The lively chatter of locals blended with the soft strumming of a ukulele nearby, the music floating through the air like a gentle caress. Kathy stopped in front of a vendor selling bright pareos, her eyes sparkling with delight as she picked up a fabric that danced in the breeze, its colors reminiscent of a sunset.

"Look at this!" she exclaimed, holding it up against her skin, the fabric flowing like water. "It's beautiful. I need to get one to remember this place."

She twirled with the fabric, her eyes beaming with excitement. "You should definitely get it. It'll be the perfect reminder of our time here."

As we continued through the market, I could feel the energy radiating from Kathy. She was alive with the spirit of the island, her joy contagious. Every stall we passed held treasures—handcrafted jewelry, fragrant spices, and paintings that captured the island's essence. We stopped frequently, drawn in by the vibrant displays and the stories of the vendors, each moment weaving together to create the fabric of our shared experience.

"Let's take a picture with that mural!" Kathy pointed to a colorful wall adorned with a stunning painting of a tropical sunset, its hues echoing the vibrancy of our surroundings.

"Great idea!" I agreed, and we moved closer, the artist's brush strokes capturing the magic of the island perfectly. We asked a local woman to help us with a photograph of the mural and us. As we posed together, her laughter filled the air, a melody I wanted to bottle up and keep forever. The moment felt infinite, suspended in time.

Kathy's eyes sparkled with mischief as she leaned in closer, whispering, "I want to remember this moment forever."

I returned her smile, "I promise to keep it alive," I said, capturing her joy in my mind. The woman snapped the photo, the camera clicking, echoing our joy.

As we wandered further, Kathy's enthusiasm grew. Each step we took seemed to weave a spell around us, a bond forged in the heart of Tahiti. The warmth of the sun above, the laughter of locals, and the beauty of the island wrapped around us like a soft embrace, urging us to savor every second.

"Today is ours," she declared, "Let's make it unforgettable."

As we approached our hotel, the Royal Tahitian, a charming boutique nestled just a few blocks from the beach, a sense of wonder washed over me. The white stucco walls gleamed under the tropical sun, their brightness almost blinding against the backdrop of the azure sky. Lush gardens surrounded the property, a riot of color bursting forth from every corner. Hibiscus and orchids flaunted their vivid petals, their colors so vibrant they almost didn't seem real, each flower a splash of joy against the greenery.

We stepped inside, a welcome relief from the heat outside. The concierge stood ready to greet us, a warm smile stretching across his face as he approached. In his hands, he held a string of leis made from fragrant gardenias, their delicate blossoms releasing a sweet perfume that filled the air like an intoxicating embrace.

"Bienvenue à Tahiti," he said, his accent thick and melodic, like the music that lingered in the air. He draped the leis around our necks, the soft petals brushing against my skin, instantly making me feel more connected to this paradise.

Kathy beamed at him, her face lighting up in a way that made my heart skip a beat. "Merci beaucoup," she replied, her voice carrying that lightness I had grown to love. There was undeniable magic about her; she always seemed to absorb the energy of a place, and here, in this island paradise, she was glowing, radiating happiness like the sun itself.

"Please, let me know if there is anything you need during your stay," the concierge continued, his demeanor warm and welcoming. "We want to ensure your time here is unforgettable."

As I glanced at Kathy, her eyes sparkling with excitement, I could see the wheels turning in her mind, already dreaming of the adventures that awaited us.

"This hotel is perfect," she murmured, her gaze sweeping over the vibrant decor and the lush greenery that spilled over the edges of the garden.

"Let's make sure we capture it all," I replied, "Photos, stories… everything."

With a soft laugh, she squeezed my hand, her eyes shining like the sun overhead. "And maybe a few souvenirs?"

"Absolutely," I grinned, imagining the treasures we would find—mementos to remind us of this incredible journey. "But for now, let's just enjoy being here."

As we stepped into our room, the sunlight poured in through the large windows, illuminating the space with a golden glow. The decor was simple yet elegant, reflecting the island's spirit—woven mats on the floor, wooden accents, and bright tropical prints that breathed life into the space.

Kathy spun around, her laughter echoing off the walls. "I love it!" she exclaimed. "It feels so... alive!"

Chuckling, I watched her dance around the room, her energy vibrant and infectious. "Just wait until we hit the beach. You'll be in paradise."

Her laughter filled the air, a melody I wanted to replay over and over. "I can't wait!"

At that moment, as I watched her embrace the spirit of the island, I felt an overwhelming sense of gratitude. We were here together, embarking on a quest that promised to be filled with joy, laughter, and unforgettable memories.

Once we were settled in our room, I threw open the balcony doors, letting the ocean breeze rush in like a salty embrace. The air carried the scent of salt and the promise of discovery, filling the space with a freshness that invigorated my senses. From where we stood, we had a perfect view of the beach—white sand stretching endlessly, meeting the turquoise waters in a seamless line that seemed to whisper tales of distant horizons. The sun hung high now, casting a golden glow over everything, making the waves sparkle like diamonds scattered across a blue silk cloth.

Kathy stepped out onto the balcony, her hair lifted gently by the breeze, strands swirling around her face in a playful dance. "It's perfect," she said, her voice barely above a whisper, filled with awe. She closed her eyes, breathing in the salty air, and I watched her features soften, the lines of stress melting away as the island worked its magic on her.

"It's beautiful, isn't it?" she murmured, her voice soft, almost reverent.

Facing her, I was captivated not just by the view but by the radiant glow of her face. The sun caught the strands of her auburn hair.

"Yes, of course," I replied, my own gaze sweeping the coastline, feeling the thrill within me. "I could get used to this."

Her lips curled into a smile, one that lit up her entire being.

"This is paradise, Bob," she said, her voice tinged with awe.

"Can you believe we're really here?" I asked.

"Such a great choice to elope, Bob!"

The sincerity in her voice struck a chord deep within me. I stepped closer, my heart swelling with emotion.

"Just promise me we'll explore this place," she said, her eyes sparkling with excitement. "I want to swim in those turquoise waters, hike those lush trails, and dance under the stars on the beach."

"No problem," I replied.

We shared a look then, a moment where everything else faded away—the WindStar, the harbor, the world beyond—and all that mattered was us.

In that instant, I realized that it wasn't just the stunning landscape that captivated me; it was the journey we were starting together. Our laughter echoed in the breeze as we leaned over the railing, soaking in the beauty that lay ahead.

She smiled at that, a small, wistful smile.

"Can we stay here forever?" she added, the longing in her tone resonating deeply within me.

Joining her, I leaned against the railing, feeling the cool metal against my palms. Together, we watched the waves roll in, the rhythmic sound a soothing melody that seemed to echo the pulse of the island. "Maybe we should," I teased, a playful smile creeping onto my lips. "Just disappear. Live on the beach, sell coconuts to tourists."

She laughed, a soft giggle that danced in the air, and in that moment, it felt like we could. It felt like the world outside this island didn't exist, and we were the only two people that mattered.

"It's clear to me," she said, her eyes sparkling with mischief. "You, with your little coconut stand, charming all the tourists with your 'authentic island vibes.'"

"Hey, I'd be great at it!" I shot back, feigning indignation. "I can be very charming when I need to be."

Kathy raised an eyebrow, her playful smile broadening. "Oh, really? Let's see it then, coconut man."

Throwing my hands up in mock surrender. "Alright, alright! But only if you promise to wear a grass skirt and dance for the customers."

Her laughter rang out again, bright and full of life, filling the air around us with warmth. It was a sound that lifted my spirits and made the world feel infinitely more expansive, as if our dreams had no limits.

Later that afternoon, we wandered down to the beach, the soft sand warm beneath our feet, like a comforting blanket that enveloped us with each step. The sun was beginning to descend, turning the sky from warm yellow to tinges of orange and pink, a canvas that seemed to ignite the very essence of the island. The sea mirrored those colors, turning the water into a shimmering palette of light, each wave a brushstroke of vibrant beauty.

As we walked along the shore, the warm sand molded beneath our toes, inviting us deeper into the enchanting atmosphere. The beach was quiet, except for a few sunbathers, their bodies sprawled on towels, soaking in the last rays of the day. I noticed a child giggling in the distance, splashing in the surf. Her laughter was a bright note that harmonized with the gentle lapping of the waves.

"Look at that!" Kathy pointed, her eyes sparkling with delight. "That little girl is having the time of her life."

Turning to her, the joy in her voice radiated like the sun overhead. "Just like us," I remarked, a grin spreading across my face.

We walked for a good while and found a group of palm trees that looked beaten and tattered from battling pacific storms. They were the ones that leaned so far they were almost on the ground. We found a spot to settle under the palms in the shade.

The sand was soft and inviting beneath us, and as we sat down, I felt an overwhelming sense of peace wash over me. I looked over at Kathy, who was gazing out at the horizon, her face radiant with the golden light of the setting sun.

Kathy shocked me as she jumped up and grabbed my hand, exclaiming, "Bob, let's go treasure hunting. Look!" she said, pointing, "I see a shiny object down the beach."

"Yeah, let's go," I shouted, as we started to run. "What do you think? Will we find Captain Hook's long-lost chest of gold?" I smirked.

"No, silly," she responded, "sea glass and beautiful, unique shells."

"You're the silly one," I said, as I pulled her into the ocean directly in the way of a huge wave.

We both came up sputtering and spitting salt water, but in her fisted hand, she proudly showed me her treasure – a beautiful sand dollar.

"You're the winner, Kathy," I playfully teased her. Grabbing her hand, I pulled her out of the water to continue her treasure hunt.

As we walked, Kathy's hand slipped into mine, her warm and reassuring touch, a perfect fit that sent a rush of contentment through me. "Do you think we'll ever come back here?" she asked, her voice thoughtful, almost wistful, as she gazed at the horizon.

Squeezing her hand slightly, "I hope so," I said, agreeing to my promise.

Kathy nodded, her eyes fixed on the horizon, reflecting the myriad shades of the sunset. "I don't want to forget this. Any of it," she confessed, her voice soft, filled with a longing that tugged at my heart.

"You won't," I promised, stopping to pull her into my arms.

The sound of the waves lapping gently at the shore wrapped around us like a soothing melody, the perfect backdrop to this intimate moment. "We'll hold onto this. All of it."

Her smile was a soft glow against the fading light, her eyes filled with an emotion that was deeper than words, a mixture of gratitude and joy.

Later that evening, we visited the hotel's pool. The pool was lit by soft, underwater lights that cast a shimmering glow over the water, transforming it into a liquid silver oasis. The first stars began to peek through the darkening sky, twinkling like tiny jewels scattered across the heavens.

The pool was nearly deserted, save for a woman floating lazily on her back, her laughter mingling with the soft sounds of the evening. The scene felt like a dreamscape, a perfect escape from reality. She was pregnant, and I chuckled as I realized she was topless too. The sight was strangely serene, almost sacred in its simplicity, embodying the tranquility of the island. Her body relaxed and free, as if she had become one with the very essence of the water around her. The soft ripples of the pool gently caressed her skin, reflecting the ambient glow of the underwater lights, creating an ethereal aura around her. Kathy stood by the edge of the pool, her eyes wide with quiet reverence, captivated by the sight.

"She looks so peaceful," Kathy whispered, her voice barely audible, as if speaking too loudly might disrupt the serenity of the moment.

"Yeah," I agreed, my gaze fixed on the woman's slow, rhythmic movements, like a graceful dance in harmony with the water. "It's like she's a part of the Tahitian Islands protruding from the beautiful Pacific Ocean."

"Shall we?" I asked, gesturing toward the inviting water.

Kathy's eyes lit up with mischief, a soft smile tugging at her lips. "Absolutely. Last one across owes the other a wish!"

She slipped into the water, barely sending a ripple across the surface. I followed, easing in beside her, careful not to disturb the delicate stillness, like we were guests on a floating dream.

The cool embrace of the water wrapped around us, serene and invigorating. We moved slowly at first, letting the night settle around us, our laughter quiet and reverent. Beneath the moon's gentle gaze, it felt as though time had paused, and in that suspended moment, Kathy shimmered—light, free, and full of wonder.

Eventually, we settled on the pool's edge, our legs dangling in the cool water, the soft glow of the underwater lights making our faces glow. I turned to her, watching as she gazed up at the stars, her expression a mix of wonder and contentment.

"Look at that one!" she exclaimed, pointing to a particularly bright star. "It's like it's shining just for us."

"Maybe it is," I said, leaning closer, feeling the warmth of her damp shoulder against mine. "Just a reminder that moments like this are special. That we're meant to be here, right now, together."

Kathy smiled, turning to me with a sparkle in her eyes. "I love that thought," she said softly. "No matter what happens, we'll always have this."

"Always," I promised, my heart swelling with love and certainty.

Kathy glanced at me, her eyes glistening with a mixture of awe and something deeper—an emotion that felt significant. "Do you ever think about...?" Her voice trailed off, leaving the question hanging in the air, heavy with meaning.

"About having kids?" I asked, turning to face her fully, drawn into the weight of the moment. "Sometimes. Do you?"

She nodded slowly, her gaze drifting back to the woman in the pool, lost in thought. "Yeah. I don't know when... or where we'll be, but... yeah. I think about it." Her voice carried a weight that spoke of dreams and uncertainties, hopes and fears.

Reaching out, I gently tucked a strand of hair behind her ear and caressed her cheek with the back of my hand. "When the time is right, we'll know," I said, my tone reassuring, wanting her to feel the certainty in my words.

Kathy smiled softly, her hand finding mine, our fingers intertwining like the roots of trees seeking nourishment from the earth. "I think so too," she replied, her voice steady and filled with warmth.

The moment stretched between us, watching as the woman floated, her belly glowing softly in the pool's light, a beacon of life and possibility. At that moment, everything felt connected—us, the island, the future we hadn't yet planned but were beginning to imagine.

The world around us faded into the background, the sounds of the night—a gentle breeze rustling through the palm trees, the soft lapping of water against the pool's edge—creating a cocoon of intimacy. I could feel the pulse of the island mirroring our own, a reminder that we were part of something greater.

"What would it be like?" Kathy pondered aloud, her eyes shining with curiosity. "To bring a little one into this world, to share all of this beauty with them?"

"Beautiful," I replied, imagining the possibilities. "To watch them explore, to see their eyes light up with wonder at the simplest things, just like we are now."

Her smile widened, a mixture of hope and excitement illuminating her face. "And to teach them about love, about adventure... about life."

"Yes," I affirmed, feeling a rush of warmth envelop us. "To show them how to chase their dreams and embrace every moment."

As the woman continued to float serenely, the water cradling her, I couldn't help but think that this was a glimpse into our own future—a future filled with love, laughter, and the promise of new beginnings. We were standing on the precipice of something beautiful, ready to dive into the depths of life together, whatever that might look like.

In that magical evening, surrounded by the tranquility of the island and the promise of tomorrow, I felt an overwhelming sense of peace settle within me.

The next morning, the sky was still tinged with the soft pastels of dawn, hues of pink and orange blending seamlessly as if nature itself were painting a masterpiece to bid us farewell. We packed our bags with a mix of reluctance and nostalgia.

"Okay," I said. "One last stop before we head home."

We made our way to the airport, and a quietness settled between us, the kind that lingers when something important is coming to an end, heavy with unspoken emotions.

Papeete's streets were still sleepy, shrouded in a gentle haze of morning mist. The early light cast long shadows across the pavement, creating an ethereal ambiance that seemed to whisper of the beauty we were leaving behind. We boarded a taxi, the interior filled with the comforting scent of leather and the faint hum of the engine, and I felt a pang of sadness wash over me.

Kathy rested her head against my shoulder in the backseat, her fingers idly tracing patterns on my arm, the touch both soothing and possessive. "It feels like we've been here forever," she murmured, "but also like it went by too fast."

Nodding, I understood exactly what she meant, the sentiment echoing within me. "Yeah. It's hard to leave, but...," I hesitated, searching for the right words to capture the bittersweet nature of our departure. "But I think we're taking a piece of it with us."

Her smile was soft, almost wistful, her eyes half-closed as she absorbed my words. "You're right. I'll carry this place with me.

Always." There was a determination in her voice that made my heart swell, a promise that we would cherish these memories wherever we went.

The flight back to Hawaii was smooth. The plane was only half full. We could pick our seats, take two or three seats, and even lie down. It was like a private jet. The plane cut through the clouds effortlessly, gliding on invisible currents as if it were part of the sky. Kathy drifted in and out of sleep beside me, her hand resting comfortably in mine, her face peaceful and serene. Outside the window, the vast Pacific stretched endlessly, a deep blue that seemed to go on forever, mirroring the boundless possibilities that awaited us when we landed.

As we soared high above the ocean, I couldn't help but steal glances at Kathy, her lashes fluttering softly against her cheeks. Each time she stirred, a small smile danced on her lips, and I felt a wave of gratitude wash over me. This journey had brought us closer and had carved out moments that would forever be etched in our memories.

When the plane touched down in Hawaii, the familiar sense of finality enveloped me, but alongside it was a spark of anticipation. We had come so far together, navigating the beauty and complexities of our love, and though this part of our journey was ending, something else was beginning.

As we got off the plane, Kathy squeezed my hand, her eyes meeting mine with that same soft smile she had worn the day we met, filled with warmth and unspoken understanding. "We made it," she said, her voice full of quiet triumph, a note of victory that resonated in my chest.

"Yeah, we did," I replied, pulling her close, the weight of the world momentarily lifting as I felt her warmth against me.

As we stepped into the vibrant energy of Hawaii, I found comfort in knowing that, together, we would explore, laugh, and share each moment, facing whatever came next.

# Chapter 11
# Crossing the Line

The airport buzzed with the rhythm of a typical evening—travelers dragging weary feet over the shiny tile floors. Announcements crackling over the PA system and the occasional clatter of luggage carts breaking through the crowd reminded us we were on our way home. We moved together, Kathy's hand nestled comfortably in mine, as we navigated the last stretch of our long journey.

"There," I said, pointing toward the customs line. "We're almost done."

My eyes sharpened as they locked onto a couple ahead of us in line. The pair seemed misplaced in the bustling airport. The man was thin, his face gaunt, his hands twitching at irregular intervals. Beside him, the woman kept adjusting her scarf, glancing around the room as if she expected someone to approach them at any moment.

"Look at those two," I muttered, my voice low. "If anyone here has something to hide, it's them."

Kathy followed my gaze and let out a soft laugh. "Bob, not everyone's a character out of a cop drama. They're probably just nervous travelers."

"Maybe." My expression didn't waver. My instincts, honed over years of business negotiations and reading people, told me otherwise. But I let it go, focusing instead on getting through customs.

"You're impossible," Kathy teased, shaking her head. "Let's just get through this."

The line shuffled forward. The nervous couple moved ahead to the customs counter, their whispered conversation growing more animated as the officer questioned them. Kathy leaned closer to me and whispered, "See, totally fine."

The moment hung in delicate balance, the mundane routine of the airport masking the subtle tension that was beginning to creep into the edges of our experience. The customs officer was tall and stoic, his gaze sharp as it swept over the crowd. His eyes flickered over us as we stepped up to the counter, lingering for just a moment longer than was comfortable.

"Random inspection," the officer said briskly, nodding toward Kathy's suitcase.

Frowning, I asked, "Is something wrong?" My voice was steady, but there was a flicker of unease in my tone.

"No," the officer replied flatly. "Just routine."

Kathy gave me a reassuring squeeze on the arm and smiled at the officer. "No problem," she said. "Take your time."

The officer's hand reached for the suitcase; his expression wasn't clear. We exchanged a glance, our earlier ease beginning to slip away.

The suitcase landed on the counter with a thud, its smooth fabric stark against the sterile, stainless steel surface. Kathy stepped back, her smile tight but polite, while I crossed my arms; my unease was growing with each passing second. The customs officer adjusted his gloves with deliberate slowness, a faint snap echoing as he tugged them into place. Around us, the bustling energy of the customs hall continued, but for Kathy and I, the world had narrowed to this one moment.

"You folks traveling together?" the officer asked, his voice calm but clinical as he unzipped the suitcase.

"Yes," I replied, the word sharp and curt. Kathy shot me a look, silently urging me to dial back the defensiveness.

"Where are you coming from?" the officer continued as his hands moved through the suitcase, flipping open neatly folded shirts and shifting pairs of sandals to the side.

"Tahiti," Kathy answered quickly, her voice steady despite the sudden knot forming in her stomach. "It was our honeymoon."

The officer didn't respond. Instead, his gloved hands slowed as they reached the center of the suitcase, brushing against the brittle, dried flowers she'd placed there. He picked them up carefully, holding the delicate bouquet aloft, his brow furrowing.

"These yours?" he asked, tilting the flowers in the light as if they might reveal a secret.

Kathy nodded. "Yes, they are a keepsake from our wedding. I wore them in my hair."

The officer paused, considering her explanation. "These should have been declared." He looked at the flowers for a moment longer before setting them aside and continuing his search. There was nothing incriminating about those flowers—nothing wrong with keeping a token from the happiest day of her life. Something about the officer's methodical movements, the way he inspected every corner of her suitcase, set her nerves on edge. Kathy gripped my arm, "Bob, I need to sit down!"

Leaning closer, I lowered my voice. "It's fine, Kath. They're just being thorough."

Though her eyes betrayed her growing unease, she whispered, "It's just…I forgot about…."

The officer's hand suddenly froze mid-search. His fingers curled around something small and square in the suitcase's front pocket. With deliberate slowness, he withdrew a matchbox, its once-bright logo now worn from handling. He held it up to the light, his gaze unreadable.

Kathy's stomach dropped.

"Is this yours too?" the officer asked, his voice neutral.

Her breath caught, and for a moment, she couldn't speak. Her mind raced, replaying that morning on the beach in Maui. The matchbox had been so small, so insignificant. She'd tossed it in her suitcase without a second thought. Now, it was here, in the hands of a customs officer.

"Yes," she said finally, her voice barely above a whisper.

The officer opened the matchbox. A faint rustling sound filled the air as he revealed the tiny, green-tinted contents within. His expression hardened.

"They found it," Kathy murmured, her voice trembling.

Frowning and leaning closer. I asked, "Found what?"

She turned to me, her face pale. "The pot," she whispered. "The pot from Maui."

The room seemed to freeze as the customs officer held the open matchbox in his hand, the contents now fully exposed. I stared at it, then at Kathy, the weight of her words settling over me like a heavy, suffocating blanket.

"You're kidding, right?" I muttered, my voice tight with disbelief. "Tell me you're joking."

Kathy's gaze didn't waver. "I didn't think—I forgot it was in there," she stammered, her voice tinged with panic. "I didn't mean to—"

"Ma'am," the officer interrupted, his tone curt but calm. He held up the matchbox. "This is marijuana. Are you admitting this is yours?"

Kathy blinked, her throat dry. For a moment, she considered lying, deflecting, anything to make this situation go away. But she knew it was futile. Her heart pounded in her chest, the sound echoing in her ears like a drumbeat.

"Yes," she said finally, her voice small but steady. "It's mine."

Running a hand down my face, my jaw tightened with frustration. "Kathy," I hissed under my breath, "what the hell were you thinking?"

She didn't answer; her eyes were glued on the customs officer as he motioned for a colleague. Another officer, a woman with a similarly stern demeanor, approached and exchanged a glance with the first.

"We'll need to bring you both for further questioning," the male officer said, his tone devoid of sympathy.

"Is this really necessary?" I asked, my voice rising slightly. "It's barely enough to fill a matchbox!"

The officer's expression didn't change. "Sir, possession of marijuana is illegal under federal law. Under the current policy, there's zero tolerance. Now, if you'll follow us."

(At the time, federal regulations still classified marijuana as a Schedule I drug, and even trace amounts were treated as a federal offense in all states, including Hawaii).

The officer had hesitated; I remember that clearly. His shoulders were stiff, his hands uncertain. "I'm sorry," he said again, softer this time, as he gently led her toward the patrol car. Kathy nodded, lips pressed tightly together, holding herself together with every ounce of strength she had.

I wanted to scream. To say something. To stop it. But what could I have possibly said? What could I have done? The law was what it was, and no amount of pleading would've changed the outcome. I just stood there, powerless.

Before I could open my mouth to protest again, Kathy touched my arm lightly, shaking her head. "Don't," she whispered. "It'll just make it worse."

The officers escorted us toward a set of side doors, their path cutting through the crowd. Travelers turned to watch, their curious stares burning into Kathy and I like a spotlight. Kathy's cheeks flushed with humiliation, but she kept her head high. I, on the other hand, looked like I was barely holding myself together from flipping out and creating a ruckus.

As we approached the police station doors, the female officer gestured for Kathy to enter a room on the left while the male officer pointed me to a room on the right. "You'll be questioned separately," she said. "Please cooperate fully."

Hesitating, my gaze darted toward Kathy. "Wait—why separate? I should be with her."

"It's standard procedure," the officer replied matter-of-factly.

Kathy squeezed my hand briefly before letting go. "It's fine," she said, though the words felt hollow. Her stomach churned as she stepped into the small, windowless room. The door closed behind her with a dull thud, and she was left with nothing but the stark fluorescent light over her head and the sound of her own breathing.

In the room across the hall, I stood frozen as the male officer gestured toward a box of rubber gloves on the table. The sight made my stomach drop. This wasn't just a misunderstanding anymore—it was the beginning of something far worse.

The sound of the door closing behind Kathy reverberated like a final, decisive note. She stood in the center of the room, her arms wrapped around herself, trying to push back the tremors in her hands. The stark light above buzzed faintly, casting harsh shadows that made the room feel even smaller. There was nothing here but a table, two metal chairs, and the heavy weight of her own thoughts.

Moments later, the female officer entered, carrying a clipboard. Her expression was neither hostile nor kind—it was simply unreadable, which made it all the more unnerving. She set the clipboard on the table and gestured for Kathy to sit.

"Mrs. Erck," the officer began, her voice calm but firm. "We're going to ask you some questions, take down your information, and document the items found in your possession. Do you understand?"

Kathy nodded mutely, her throat too dry to form words.

"Speak up, please," the officer said, her pen poised over the clipboard.

"Yes," Kathy croaked, then cleared her throat. "Yes, I understand."

Across the hall, I was having a very different experience. The male customs officer was rifling through my belongings with a precision that felt almost surgical. I stood stiffly in the corner, my fists clenched, my jaw ticking with barely contained frustration.

"Look, this is a mistake," I said, breaking the silence. "It wasn't intentional. Do you really think we're drug smugglers? Look at us!"

The officer barely glanced at me. "Sir, this isn't about intent. It's about the law."

"The law? I let out a humorless laugh. "It's not like she's carrying bricks of cocaine! It's barely a speck. What are you going to do? Charge her with smuggling?"

The officer stopped what he was doing and fixed me with a pointed stare. "Yes," he said simply. "That's exactly what we're going to do."

The words hit me like a physical blow. For a moment, I couldn't speak; the weight of the situation came crashing over me. I had heard about Reagan's zero-tolerance drug policies—how even the smallest infraction could lead to devastating consequences. But I had never imagined Kathy and I would find ourselves caught in its crosshairs.

Back in her room, Kathy was grappling with the reality of those consequences. The officer had taken her passport and license, placing them in a clear plastic bag along with the matchbox. The sight of her name printed so neatly on the confiscated items made everything feel terrifyingly official.

"We'll also need your fingerprints," the officer said, motioning to an ink pad on the table.

Kathy hesitated, her stomach twisting. "Is that really necessary?"

"Yes," the officer replied, her tone leaving no room for argument.

As Kathy pressed her fingers into the ink, she felt a surge of anger rise within her—at herself, the absurdity of the situation, the laws that turned a minor infraction into a major criminal offense just wasn't fair. But the anger was quickly swallowed by fear. What would happen next? What would this mean for her, for Bob, for their future?

My patience, on the other hand, had finally snapped. "This is ridiculous," I said, my voice rising. "You can't treat us like criminals for this. We just got married, for God's sake!"

The officer remained unfazed. "Sir, yelling isn't going to help your case."

Biting back a retort took all my effort. I glanced at the box of rubber gloves on the table and felt a fresh wave of dread. What else were they planning to do? How far was this going to go?

The door opened suddenly, and another officer stepped in, motioning for the first officer to step outside. They exchanged hushed words in the hallway; their voices were too low for me to make out their conversation. When the original officer returned, his expression had hardened.

"We need to wrap this up quickly," he said, his tone brisk. "There's more going on than you realize."

My stomach sank. "What do you mean? More is going on?"

The officer didn't answer. Instead, he gestured for me to sit. "Let's focus on the matter at hand."

The cold detachment of the officer's words sent a chill through me. Whatever 'more' meant, it was clearly not in our favor.

Kathy's hands trembled as she wiped the ink residue off her fingers with the paper towel provided. The fingerprints had been taken, her passport and license sealed in a plastic evidence bag, and the matchbox sat ominously on the table between her and the customs officer. Each step felt like a chisel carving into the reality of her life, turning what should have been a mundane flight home into a spiraling nightmare.

"We need to explain the charges," the officer said, flipping through a laminated handbook on the table. Her voice remained clinical, devoid of judgment but also lacking. "You are being charged with possession of an illegal substance and possibly smuggling. Under the Zero-Tolerance Drug Act, these charges are mandatory, regardless of the amount or intent."

Kathy stared at the officer, disbelief flickering across her face. "Smuggling?" she repeated, her voice hollow. "That's absurd. It was a matchbox with a tiny bit of marijuana. I wasn't smuggling anything."

The officer didn't look up. "The law defines smuggling as transporting controlled substances across borders, regardless of quantity or personal use. Under current federal guidelines, enforcement has zero discretion. Zero tolerance means zero exceptions."

Kathy slumped back in her chair, the weight of the words pressing down on her. Her mind spun with questions and half-formed protests, but none of them felt substantial enough to break through the iron wall of bureaucracy she was facing. "This can't be happening," she muttered, more to herself than to anyone else.

On the other side of the hall, I was pacing again, my frustration mounting with every passing second. "I want to see my wife," I said sharply. "You've separated us for what? To intimidate us?"

The officer leaned back against the door, arms crossed. "Sir, your wife has admitted to possession. We're following protocol. You're free to wait here quietly, or we can escort you to a holding cell. Your choice."

Realizing I had become argumentative, I paused, my fists still clenched at my sides. I wanted to lash out, to demand answers, but Kathy's face flashed before my eyes—her quiet strength, her ability to hold steady even in chaos. I forced myself to take a breath, to channel my energy into understanding the situation. "So, what happens now?" I asked, my voice low and tense.

The officer gave a slight shrug, the indifference in the gesture grating against my frayed nerves. "She'll be processed. Charges will be filed. Depending on the circumstances, she may face additional penalties. That's up to the federal court system."

My stomach turned. I thought of Kathy, alone in that cold, sterile room, enduring this nightmare with no idea how far it would go. My mind raced back to the days of news reports about Reagan's zero-tolerance policies. I remembered stories of people's lives being upended over minor violations, sentences that far outweighed the crime.

"You can't be serious," I said, my voice barely above a whisper. "This is our honeymoon, for crying out loud. We're not criminals."

The officer's eyes softened for the first time, but his words were no less firm. "Sir, the agents here don't make the laws. We just enforce them. And under current federal guidelines, this is mandatory."

Back in her room, Kathy felt the same grim realization settling over her. She pressed her hands flat against the cool surface of the table. She thought of Bob, his fierce protectiveness, and how much she hated that he had to see her like this. She also knew something else: no matter how scared she was, she couldn't let him take the blame for her mistake.

"If you're going to charge someone," Kathy said suddenly, her voice cutting through the sterile silence of the room. "Charge me. The pot is mine. Not Bob's. He didn't even know about it."

The officer glanced up, surprised by the force in her voice. "We understand, Mrs. Erck. Your husband isn't under investigation. This is solely about your possession and intent to transport."

*Intent to transport.* The words sounded absurd in her ears. She wanted to scream, to toss the chair across the room, to make someone understand how ridiculous this all was. Instead, she sat still, her pulse racing, her thoughts spinning.

"We'll complete the processing shortly," the officer said, gathering the paperwork. "You'll be booked and taken to a holding area until further instructions. Once the formal charges are filed, you'll be required to appear in court."

Kathy blinked, her throat dry. "And then what?"

The officer didn't answer directly. Instead, she gestured toward the door. "For now, let's take it one step at a time."

Kathy stood slowly, her knees threatening to buckle. One step at a time, she repeated to herself. With each step, the enormity of what was happening grew heavier.

Across the hall, the door to my room opened, and a different officer stepped inside. "We need to talk about Kathy's situation," he said gravely.

Turning sharply, my breath caught. "What's going on?"

The officer's expression was impossible to interpret. "It's complicated. And we have a serious problem."

# Chapter 12
# The Separation

Kathy's heart sank as she was led out of the interrogation room and down a barren hallway. The walls were bare except for the occasional security camera, its red light blinking ominously, reminding her that there was no privacy in this nightmare. Her feet dragged slightly, the weight of what was happening pressing harder with each step.

"Where are you taking me?" she finally asked, her voice unsteady.

"To the holding area," the officer replied without looking back. "It's a temporary space until the next stage of processing."

The words offered no comfort. Kathy glanced over her shoulder, hoping for a glimpse of Bob, but the hallway was empty. She hadn't seen him since they'd been separated, and her stomach churned with worry about what he was going through. Was he angry? Scared? Both? She couldn't shake the image of his face when the officer found the marijuana in her suitcase- the disbelief, the frustration, and the fear that had clouded his eyes.

The officer led her into a small holding room, its cold, gray walls closing in around her. There was a metal bench bolted to the floor and a single, harsh overhead light that buzzed faintly. The officer motioned for her to sit, then left without another word; the heavy door clicked shut behind him. The sound echoed in the small space, leaving Kathy alone with her thoughts.

She pulled her knees to her chest and rested her head on them, trying to steady her breathing. Her mind raced, replaying every decision that had led to this moment. The matchbox on the beach, the laughter and ease of that morning—it felt like a lifetime ago. Now, that tiny indulgence had spiraled into something unimaginable.

In a separate room, my anxiety had boiled into a mix of frustration and helplessness. The officer standing across from me had just uttered the words that made my heart sink. "It's complicated, we have a serious problem."

"What does that mean? What's happening to my wife?" I stepped closer, my voice tight.

The officer sighed, glancing at the clipboard in his hands. "Your wife is being charged with possession and possibly smuggling under federal drug laws. Routinely, small quantities like this wouldn't escalate so severely, but President Reagan's zero-tolerance policies in place leave no room for discretion."

I felt my insides tighten. "She's not a smuggler. This is absurd. It was a tiny amount. You know it wasn't intentional."

"Yes, I understand that, sir," the officer said, his tone softening slightly, "but the law doesn't. Once the charges are filed, it's out of our hands."

My mind raced through every possible scenario. I shook my head, pacing the room. I could see Kathy's face—her brave, composed expression even as she admitted to the matchbox being hers. My chest tightened with guilt. How had I not noticed it before?

How had I not thought to double-check everything before we went through customs?

Turning back to the officer, I pleaded. "There has to be something we can do. A fine, a warning, something other than ruining her life over this."

The officer looked at me for a long moment before speaking. "I understand your frustration. I truly do. However, right now, the best thing you can do is stay calm and be there for her. You both need to cooperate fully. It's the only way to keep this situation from escalating further."

Just as I opened my mouth to argue, the door behind the officer opened, and another agent stepped in. They exchanged a brief, hushed conversation before the first officer turned back to me.

"You'll be allowed to see her shortly," he said. "But there are procedures we need to complete first."

Swallowing the lump in my throat, I nodded. I wanted to shout, to demand they let me see Kathy now, but I knew it wouldn't help. Instead, I sank into the chair at the edge of the room, running a hand through my hair. My mind swirled with questions and fears, but one thought rose above the chaos: I had to fix this.

***

In the holding room, Kathy stared at the door, her legs shaking nervously. The air felt thick and oppressive, as if the walls were closing in. Time moved painfully slow, each minute stretching into an eternity. She thought of Bob, imagining him pacing, worrying, trying to figure out what to do. She hated that he was being dragged into this. It was her mistake, her responsibility, and yet here they were, both trapped in a nightmare of her making.

The door finally opened, and the same officer from earlier entered, her expression cryptic. "You'll be moved shortly," she said. "But before that, do you have anything else you'd like to declare? Anything you may have forgotten?"

Kathy shook her head quickly. "No. That was the only thing, I swear."

The officer nodded but didn't respond. She stepped out again, leaving Kathy alone once more. Kathy buried her face in her hands, her mind racing. She had no idea what was coming next, but its weight pressed heavily on her mind.

And then, somewhere deep in the building, she heard a door slam, which made her shudder. Hurried footsteps followed the sound, voices too low to make out, and the distant hum of tension in the air.

Something was happening. Whatever it was, she could feel it closing in.

Kathy's legs felt heavy as she was led down yet another empty hallway, this one darker and colder than the last. The female officer walked beside her but didn't say a word. Her silence amplified the sound of her own footsteps. Each step echoed faintly. Ahead, she saw another door—metal, reinforced, and intimidating. She couldn't help but wonder what lay on the other side.

The officer pushed the door open, revealing a room that felt even more clinical than the others. A booking station, complete with a fingerprint scanner, a desk littered with forms, and an intimidating mugshot camera mounted on a tripod. The fluorescent lights buzzed faintly, their harsh glow casting deep shadows across the bare walls.

"Stand here," the officer said, motioning to a spot marked on the floor with yellow tape. Her voice was clipped, almost mechanical, as if she had repeated this same instruction countless times before.

Kathy obeyed, her movements stiff and robotic. She tried to keep her breathing steady. Her chest felt tight, each inhale shallow and shaky. The officer turned to a nearby table, where her passport, license, and the now-infamous matchbox sat sealed in a plastic evidence bag. Seeing her personal items treated like contraband sent a fresh wave of humiliation coursing through her.

"Face forward," the officer instructed.

Kathy looked up at the camera, its lens unblinking and unfeeling. She tried to compose herself, the fear and embarrassment etched into her features were impossible to mask. The camera clicked, and the flash momentarily blinded her. She blinked rapidly, fighting the sting of tears.

As the officer worked, she spoke in a monotone voice. "You're being charged with possession of a controlled substance and possibly smuggling. These are federal charges under the Zero-Tolerance Drug Act. Do you understand?"

Kathy swallowed hard, her throat dry. "Yes," she managed to say, though the word felt foreign in her mouth. She wanted to scream, to argue, to demand they understand how absurd this was. But she knew it would make no difference.

"Do you have any medical conditions we should be aware of?" the officer continued.

"No," she replied, shaking her head.

"Do you have legal representation, or do you need one appointed to you?"

Her breath hitched at the mention of legal representation. This wasn't just a bad dream—this was real, and was escalating fast. "I... I don't know yet," she stammered. "I'll have to talk to my husband."

The officer didn't acknowledge her response. She simply finished the mugshot process and then handed her a clipboard with several forms to sign. She scanned the dense, legalistic text, but her eyes couldn't focus. The words blurred together, their meaning lost in the haze of her anxiety. Feeling overwhelmed, Kathy dropped her head in hopes of dispelling the woozy feeling overtaking her.

"Sign at the bottom," the officer said, tapping the page with her pen. Kathy hesitated for a moment before scribbling her name, her hand trembling.

Once the forms were completed, the officer said, "Follow me."

She led her to yet another room—this one even smaller, with a single bench bolted to the floor. She was directed to sit, and the door was closed behind her with a heavy clang. The sound was so final, so absolute, that it felt like the world had been sealed off entirely.

Kathy sat alone, her hands clasped tightly in her lap. She stared at the scuffed metal bench, her mind racing. She thought of Bob, wondering if he was still in the building, if he was fighting for her, or pacing in frustration. She thought of the officer's words—"federal charges," "smuggling," "zero tolerance"—each phrase looping in her mind like a broken record.

She had never felt so fragile, so powerless. The reality of what was happening crashed over her in waves, each one heavier than the last. The honeymoon glow that had once surrounded her felt like a distant memory now, replaced by the cold, brutal truth of her current situation.

In a small, sharp moment of defiance, Kathy straightened her back and lifted her chin. This wasn't how her story was going to end, she told herself. She had to hold on, to stay strong—for herself, for Bob, for the life they had promised to build together. As the minutes ticked by and no one came for her, the fragile confidence crumbled once again.

Beyond the thick, metal door, all she could hear was the faint hum of voices, too muffled to decipher. Every now and then, a door would slam, the sound making her flinch despite herself. The waiting was unbearable, each second stretching into an eternity.

Just as she felt the walls closing in, the door opened abruptly. Kathy looked up, her heart racing, but it wasn't Bob who entered. It was another officer, his face grim.

"Mrs. Erck," he said, his tone clipped. "We've finished the initial booking. You'll be held until further notice."

"Can I see my husband?" she asked, her voice trembling.

The officer hesitated. "Not yet," he said. "But he's here. He's being briefed on the situation."

Kathy nodded. At least Bob was still nearby. For now, that was enough to keep her composed.

The officer left. Kathy closed her eyes, leaning back against the cold wall. The next step was a mystery, but she knew one thing for sure: this nightmare was far from over.

\*\*\*

My foot tapped an unsteady rhythm against the cold tile floor. I sat in a cramped, fluorescent-lit waiting area. The room felt oppressive, not just because of its stark design but because of the weight of what was happening beyond its walls. Every few minutes, a police officer or security guard would pass through the room, their footsteps echoing faintly in the otherwise heavy silence. None of them acknowledged me, which only made my frustration mount and the feeling of isolation paramount.

As I ran my hands through my hair, I found myself leaning forward, elbows resting on my knees. My thoughts were a chaotic jumble of anger, guilt, and helplessness. Kathy's face was burned into my mind—the way she'd looked at me when she admitted the marijuana was hers. I hadn't understood its gravity at the moment, but now it hit me like a freight train.

How could such a small incident spiral into something this catastrophic?

The officer's words echoed in my head: "Federal charges… zero-tolerance… smuggling." It all felt so surreal. A honeymoon souvenir—a matchbox with barely enough marijuana to roll a single joint had turned into a legal nightmare that could alter our lives forever. Clenching my fists, I fought the urge to punch something. It wouldn't help Kathy, and it certainly wouldn't help me, but the anger simmering inside me was almost unbearable.

The wall clock seemed to mock me as I periodically glanced at it. The second hand ticked forward with excruciating slowness as if taunting me. I had no idea what was happening to Kathy—if she was scared, if she was okay, if she was blaming herself as much as I was blaming myself.

"If I'd checked the bags," I muttered under my breath. "If I'd just been more careful…"

The thought gnawed at me. I had been so focused on getting through customs and keeping the trip on track that I hadn't thought to double-check everything. I noticed her putting the flowers in her suitcase, but hadn't thought twice about it. And the matchbox? It hadn't even crossed my mind.

A low hum of voices outside the room caught my attention, and I sat up, straining to hear. The words were muffled, indistinct, but there was an urgency to the tone that made my pulse quicken. Was it about Kathy? Was she okay? Or was this whole thing escalating even further?

The door to the waiting area swung open, and I stood abruptly, my heart pounding. A customs officer stepped inside, his expression difficult to read. I crossed the room in a few strides, unable to wait for the officer to speak.

"What's happening?" I demanded. "Is my wife okay?"

The officer raised a hand, gesturing for me to calm down. "She's fine," he said evenly. "We've completed her booking, and she's being held for further processing."

"Processing?" I repeated, my voice rising. "What does that even mean? How long is this going to take?"

The officer hesitated, his gaze shifting slightly. "It depends," he admitted. "Right now, there are a few procedural hurdles we need to clear, but I need you to understand something, Mr. Erck. The charges against your wife are serious. This isn't something we can just wave away."

The floor seemed to drop out from under me. "You're telling me she could... what? Go to jail? Over this?"

The officer didn't answer directly. Instead, he said, "The best thing you can do right now is stay calm and cooperate. Getting angry won't help her."

"Getting angry?" I snapped. "I'm not angry—I'm terrified! Do you have any idea what this is doing to her? To us?"

The officer's expression softened slightly, but he still maintained a professional distance. "I get it," he said quietly. "I've seen this kind of situation before, and I know it's hard. But lashing out won't change the outcome. Let us do our jobs."

Feeling off balance, I stepped back, my chest heaving with barely suppressed emotion. I wanted to scream, to demand answers, to force someone to fix this. Deep down, I knew the officer was right. This was way out of my hands now, and that realization was the hardest part to accept.

As the officer turned to leave, he paused in the doorway. "We'll let you see her soon," he said. "In the meantime, try to focus on what comes next. You'll need to think about legal representation."

The door closed with a soft click, leaving me alone once again. I sank back into the chair, my hands trembling. My mind raced with questions, fears, and desperate hopes. The thought of Kathy sitting alone in some cold, lifeless room was almost too much to bear.

My eyes blurred as I looked at the clock again. Time moved forward, second by agonizing second, but for me, it felt like the world was standing still.

The door swung open, jolting me out of my spiraling thoughts. I turned quickly, expecting to see Kathy, but instead, it was another police officer. My heart sank. I braced myself, gripping the edge of the chair to steady my trembling hands.

"Mr. Erck," the officer said, stepping into the room. His tone was neutral, almost clinical, but there was an edge to it that made my pulse quicken. "We need to talk about Kathy's situation."

My voice was tight with impatience. "What's going on? Is she okay?" My legs cramped from sitting too long, so I stood.

The officer hesitated—a pause so small it might have gone unnoticed by anyone less desperate for answers. "She's being held for further questioning," he said finally. "But there's... a complication."

The word hit me like a punch to the gut. "What kind of complication?" I demanded, my voice rising. "What aren't you telling me?"

The officer stepped further into the room, closing the door behind him. His expression remained calm, but there was a flicker of something in his eyes—unease, perhaps, or something heavier. "Mr. Erck," he began, his voice low, "The decision has been made, we are charging your wife with smuggling and possession of drugs."

My mind struggled to process the words.

"Well, I understand this is a shock," the officer said, his tone softening slightly. The room spun. I stared at the officer, my mouth opening and closing as I tried to form words. "You think she's smuggling drugs? That's insane."

The officer's face remained neutral. "We're just following the law," he said. My legs gave out, and I sank back into the chair. My heart was pounding so loudly I could barely hear my own thoughts. "You're wrong," I said weakly.

The officer remained standing, his posture stiff. "We'll keep you updated as soon as we know more. For now, I suggest contacting legal counsel. This situation has the potential to become very serious."

The officer paused at the door, but he didn't turn around. "I understand this is difficult," he said. "But I suggest you prepare for what's coming."

The door closed with a heavy thud, leaving me alone in the room. My mind was spinning, my body trembling. The thought of Kathy—my Kathy—being accused of smuggling was too much to bear. I tried to focus, to think logically, but every attempt was swallowed by the growing fear in my heart.

Forcing myself to breathe, I clenched my fists. "This isn't over," I muttered, my voice steadying. "I won't let them do this to her."

As I stared at the clock on the wall, a chilling thought crept into my mind: *This situation has the potential of becoming very serious.*

# Chapter 13
# Three Days in Waiting

For hours, I stayed at the station, well into the night, as the authorities 'sorted things out.' No one offered answers, only vague reassurances that it was being handled. I was never allowed to see Kathy—not once during that long, terrifying night. I asked. I pleaded, but their rules were unyielding. They said it wasn't permitted and that everything had to follow protocol. I sat alone in the deserted waiting area, watching officers move in and out, hoping one of them would suddenly turn with good news or offer some clarity. None did.

By the time the morning light began to filter through the high, narrow windows of the station, I had been awake for what felt like days. That's when the officer finally entered the room and, in a calm but firm voice, addressed me from across the counter.

"Mr. Erck, I understand your concern, but there's nothing more we can do today. You'll need to come back tomorrow if you have further questions. Mrs. Erck will remain in custody until her court appearance in three days."

Naturally, I opened my mouth to argue, to plead. The officer's steady gaze, however, made it clear there was no room for negotiation. Defeated, I nodded silently, letting the weight of those words settle heavily on my shoulders. I turned and walked toward the exit, my footsteps echoing in the quiet corridor.

The heavy steel door shut behind me as I stepped out of the police station and into the early-morning sun. The warm Hawaiian breeze brushed my face, carrying the scent of saltwater and hibiscus, it did little to loosen the knot in my gut. My steps felt heavier than usual as I made my way to the street, replaying the officer's words in my head: *She'll have to stay in custody until her court appearance. If the judge agrees, she can be released in three days.*

Pausing on the station's steps, I glanced down at the cracked pavement beneath my feet. The bustling sounds of the island surrounded me—cars driving by, the distant chatter of tourists, and the occasional squawk of a seabird. Yet, to me, it all seemed muffled, like I was moving through water.

I originally walked into the station a day ago with the hope that some mistake had been made, that I'd be able to take Kathy home with me that very day. Instead, I was walking out alone, carrying the weight of uncertainty on my shoulders. My heart felt heavy, each beat echoing the officer's words.

"Three days," I muttered under my breath, my voice barely audible above the street noise. "How am I supposed to wait three days?"

I walked toward the curb, and the scent of blooming flowers drifted through the air. Usually that fragrance would've reminded me of the beauty of this place, but today, it only made me feel the distance between Kathy and I more sharply. I stopped for a moment.

"I'll get through this," I muttered to myself. "I have to."

The first thing I needed to do was find a rental car and a decent place to stay. Just outside the police station, I spotted a row of payphones mounted to the wall under a faded awning. Next to them was a metal shelf holding a well-worn local phone book, its cover curled from the humidity and years of use.

As I flipped through the pages, I ignored the occasional curious glance from passersby. I found a rental car agency a couple of blocks away. I fed a few coins into the phone and called ahead to reserve something simple. Having a car meant I could freely move around and look for options to help Kathy.

"This should work," I muttered as I jotted down the agency's name and address.

As I tucked the paper into my pocket, I grabbed my bag and took one last look around. The weight of the past night still clung to me, but at least now I had a plan, even a small one, and that brought me a flicker of hope.

While walking the few blocks to the rental office, the fresh air helped clear my mind. The bustling energy of Maui wrapped around me; a jarring contrast to the gloom I carried inside. The bright morning sun lit up the sidewalks, where couples strolled hand in hand, their faces glowing with joy and anticipation. I heard children's laughter echoing as they darted ahead of their parents, their carefree giggles ringing out like a melody I couldn't bring myself to join.

Shopkeepers were arranging vibrant displays of tropical fruits and souvenirs. I disregarded their cheerful greetings floating through the air as they generously welcomed passersby. Their friendliness made me feel more isolated. My internal battle took center stage; it was a storm no one else could see.

Up ahead, a group of surfers caught my eye. They were gathered on the edge of the sidewalk, waxing their boards under the golden morning sun. Their easy laughter drifted toward me—snippets of jokes, casual talk about the next wave. Normally, I might have stopped to soak in their laid-back energy, maybe even struck up a conversation. Today, however, the world felt like it belonged to someone else. It was a reminder of the ease and freedom Kathy and I had come here searching for, now feeling so far out of reach.

Then my gaze landed on one of them, and my stomach twisted. It was the guy who sold Kathy the pot. The sight of him hit me like a wave—sudden, and heavy. He was a reminder of the choices that had led us to this point.

My first instinct was to get in his face and give him a piece of my mind—but then I stopped myself. What good would it do? It wouldn't change a thing. I needed to stay focused on the real problem.

My need to persist for the sake of Kathy forced my attention back to the task at hand. My fists clenched for a moment before I shook them out, trying to dispel the cloud that hovered over me. "Just get the car," I muttered under my breath, my voice swallowed by the noise of the busy street. "One step at a time. That's all I can do."

The rental office was a small, bright building tucked between a coffee shop and a souvenir store. Its cheerful exterior—turquoise and white—stood out. I pushed open the glass door, and the cool air-conditioning washed over me, a welcome relief from the relentless Hawaiian heat. The gentle hum of the AC mixed with the soft island music playing over the speakers, creating a strangely serene atmosphere.

Behind the counter stood a young woman with a practiced smile. Her name tag read 'Lani.' She looked up as I walked in, her expression instantly brightening. "Good morning! How can I help you?" she asked, her voice warm, full of that effortless island kindness.

Her tone was genuine; I could tell, but it felt out of sync with everything I was dealing with.

Stepping up to the counter, I leaned in, setting my wallet down beside me. "I called about 20 minutes ago in hopes of renting a small car. Something simple… just to get me around for the next few days."

Lani nodded and reached for a stack of paper forms beside the register. "We've got a compact sedan available. It's efficient and easy to park, great for getting around the island," she said with the kind of polished enthusiasm that made it clear she'd delivered the line a hundred times before.

"That sounds great, thank you."

She slid the rental agreement across the counter, along with a pen. I barely glanced at the terms and conditions as she pointed out the basics—insurance coverage, gas policy, and return location. My thoughts were wrapped in a relentless loop of what-ifs and what-nows. Once I signed, she tore off the carbon copy and stamped the top sheet. She handed me a set of keys along with the rental agreement and a printed island map that had already been creased from being folded a dozen times before.

While opening the map, I asked Lani if she knew of a decent cottage or rental not too far out of the way, preferably with a view of the ocean. She thought for a moment and suggested a few rentals, 4 or 5 miles north on the main road.

Taking the map back from me, she said, tapping the highlighted route. "You'll be heading north for about ten minutes to the main highway. It should be smooth sailing from there."

Turning, I nodded a thank you and moved toward the parking lot, with the keys and a map in hand.

The small sedan, practical and unassuming, sat gleaming under a group of palm trees. I climbed in, the cool leather seats offering a brief moment of relief. I adjusted the mirrors, started the engine, and for a second, the soft hum beneath me was almost comforting. It was a small reminder that at least one thing had gone smoothly today.

Within minutes, I was navigating the unfamiliar streets of Maui. The engine purred quietly, and I found myself letting out a long-held breath. My body relaxed into the plush leather seat. My senses took in the beauty surrounding me—the swaying palms, the bursts of bougainvillea, and the shimmer of the ocean in the distance.

Lani was right, it was an easy drive to the highway. Deciding I needed to pinpoint one of her suggestions, I pulled off to the side of the road, parking beneath the shade of a tall palm. The breeze rustled the fronds above, casting slow, swaying shadows across the dashboard. I let out a long breath, then reached for the stack of brochures in the glove compartment left behind by previous renters. Most of the brochures were sun-bleached, folded and refolded, but still legible enough to serve their purpose.

As I flipped through the pages, scanning the ads and listings, I hoped for something that didn't scream honeymooners or tourist trap. Most were oversized resorts with beachfront patios and champagne welcome baskets—places Kathy would have loved, and places that now felt painfully out of place.

Then I saw it. A small ad, printed in plain type with a modest photo: a boutique hotel perched on a cliff, whitewashed walls and wooden balconies overlooking the ocean. Nothing flashy. Just simple, quiet charm. Guests described it as peaceful, secluded, serene, a place to unwind. That was what I needed more than anything. A place where the sound of the waves might drown out the chaos still pounding in my head.

It was just a short drive up the coast.

Noticing a payphone outside a grocery store, I headed for it. I fed a few coins into the slot and dialed the hotel. The woman on the other end had a kind voice and said they had a room available. "Please reserve the room for me," I responded, thanking her. I returned to the car. For the first time in hours, I felt a flicker of relief.

Resting my head against the headrest, I leaned back in my seat. For a moment, I pictured myself standing on that balcony, the sea breeze brushing against my face. "This might work," I murmured, gripping the steering wheel again. With a long breath, I started the car, holding on to the hope that this little detour might offer a sliver of peace.

The hotel was everything the photo had promised—and more. Tucked away from the noise and buzz of the tourist centers, it had an understated beauty that felt almost sacred. The whitewashed walls gleamed in the Hawaiian sun, and the lush greenery surrounding the place made it feel like it had grown straight out of the cliffside.

A row of tall palms framed the edge of the property, their fronds swaying gently in the breeze, casting shifting shadows over the stone paths that wound through the grounds. For the first time since everything had gone wrong, I felt like I could exhale—just a little.

After pulling into the small parking lot, I turned off the car. For a moment, I just sat there, letting the stillness settle around me. The sound of the waves drifted in through the open window—a steady, soothing melody that almost made me forget the chaos that had brought me here. Almost.

I stepped out into the warm air, popped open the trunk and grabbed my bag. The scent of salt and tropical flowers lingered in the breeze. I walked into the lobby, where the reception area struck a perfect balance between simplicity and elegance. A kind-eyed clerk greeted me with a warm smile. Check-in was quick, polite, and efficient—the kind of seamless process that usually put me at ease.

Moments later, I was climbing the stairs to my room on the second floor. The wooden steps creaked softly beneath my feet. The room, just like the photos, was bright and airy. Clean white linens, light wood furniture, and a quiet, lived-in coziness, which was exactly what I needed.

My eyes were drawn to the window—the real centerpiece. It offered a sweeping view of the ocean, its surface shimmering under the midday sun, stretching endlessly toward the horizon. I stood there soaking in the view, marveling at its beauty. The view felt like a gift, setting my mind at ease.

Upon setting my bag down on the bed, I walked to the window and pressed my hand gently against the glass.

The rhythmic crash of the waves filled the room with a calming sensation. "Beautiful," I whispered, breathing in the fresh salt air, knowing that Kathy would enjoy this as much as I.

Turning away from the window, I sat down heavily at the edge of the bed, staring at my hands as the full weight of the day settled on my shoulders once again.

Walking over to the balcony door, I slid open the door. The salty breeze swept over me, tousling my hair and cooling my skin as I stepped outside. I closed my eyes and let the crashing sound of the ocean fill my senses, trying to center myself before making a call.

Inside the room, I picked up the hotel's rotary phone from the nightstand. I dialed the number for home, my fingers slow on the familiar digits. It only rang twice before a familiar voice answered.

"Hello?"

"Hey, Christine, it's me," I said, doing my best to keep my tone light. "Just wanted to let you know, your sister and I've decided to extend our stay."

"Extend your stay?" she replied, surprise slipping in her voice. "Wow, you must be really loving Hawaii."

Letting out a soft, forced laugh. "Yeah, it's… it's beautiful here. We figured a few extra days wouldn't hurt."

"Well, good for you two! You deserve the break. Just make sure to take lots of pictures!"

"Will do," I said, even as my chest tightened the moment I hung up.

Lying wasn't part of who I am, but the truth felt too complicated to try explaining over a long-distance call from a hotel balcony thousands of miles away.

Briefly, I sat on the edge of the bed, staring at the receiver in my hand. Then I set it back down on the cradle and rubbed my hands over my face, trying to ease the tension that had settled there.

There was one more call I needed to make—the one I'd been dreading. I picked the receiver back up, pulled the slip of paper with the number from my wallet, and slowly dialed the Maui Police Department.

"Maui Police Department, how can I help you?" The receptionist's voice was calm, businesslike.

"Hi, this is Bob Erck. My wife, Kathy, was taken into custody yesterday morning. I'm trying to find out when she can be released."

There was a brief pause as she checked the records. "Yes, your case is scheduled for court in three days. She will remain in custody until her hearing. After that, the judge will decide whether she can be released."

"Three days?" My voice rose despite my effort to stay composed. "Is there any way to speed this up?"

"Very sorry, sir, but that's the earliest available court date. I assure you, this is standard procedure."

Exhaling slowly, my grip tightened on the phone. "Alright. One more thing… would you be able to give me the phone number for the courthouse for a recommendation for an attorney?"

"Yes, sir, one moment. It's 555-244-2728."

"Thank you," I hung up and sat down heavily on the edge of the bed. Three days. The words echoed in my mind like a sentence I couldn't escape. It wasn't the answer I'd been hoping for. I knew the answer, but I had to try to get through to someone else at the police station.

In calling the courthouse, their recommendation was Mr. Garrison, considered one of the best. With no hesitation, I called his office. His receptionist was highly professional and nice, relaying to me that Mr. Garrison would be happy to look into our case.

The hard part would be figuring out how to fill those endless hours until I could see Kathy again.

The next morning, I woke early, the restless night still clinging to me. I felt groggy and raw. I'd tried everything that night to distract myself. Flipping through the channels on the TV, skimming the book I'd brought, even pacing along the beach, but nothing could silence the gnawing worry in my chest.

After a quick breakfast at the hotel café, I decided to head back to the beach, hoping the sound of the waves might bring some kind of peace.

As I walked along the shore, the soft sand shifting beneath my feet, I replayed the events of the day before. I kept seeing Kathy's face when they took her away—the fear in her eyes, the confusion. What would I say to Kathy when I finally see her again?

Staring at the ocean brought some calmness to my pulsating heart, its vastness stretching endlessly before me—a sharp reminder of how small and powerless I felt. Then I reminded myself: this was temporary. Kathy was strong, and so was I. We'd been through challenges before, and we'd get through this one, too.

Over the next few days, I slipped into a routine. Each morning, I called the police department, hoping for some kind of update, though the answer was always the same. Afterward, I'd try to keep moving, driving through lush rainforests and winding along coastal roads. The beauty of Hawaii was undeniable. It didn't erase the worry constantly gnawing at me, but it offered moments of peace. Sometimes that was enough.

At night, I sat out on the balcony, and the sound of the waves was my only companion. I spent those quiet hours planning for the court date, jotting down questions I needed to ask, and making notes on what to say. I wrote down everything and rehearsed each word, leaving no room for error. Each list I made felt like a small way to reclaim control, like I was doing something tangible in a situation completely out of my hands.

On the third morning, I woke with a sense of resolve. Today was the day.

As I walked out of the hotel and slid into the driver's seat, I paused for a deep breath. The waiting was over. Now it was time to bring Kathy home.

# Chapter 14
# A Test of Resilience

Gripping the steering wheel tightly as I drove toward the courthouse, my jaw clenched with determination. The rising sun cast a pale golden glow over the sleepy streets, but its warmth barely touched the cold knot of anxiety lodged in my chest. I had replayed the events leading to this moment so many times I'd lost count— each decision, each misstep looping through my mind like a broken record. Could I have done something differently during the search of our luggage? Should I have spoken up more forcefully? Pushed harder? The questions haunted me; their answers were always just out of reach.

The quiet hum of the engine filled the car, but my thoughts were far louder. I could still hear the officer's voice from that night, calm but resolute: *"I don't want to arrest her, but I have no choice."* Then came the explanation, sharp and final: *"The Reagans changed the drug law to zero tolerance... anything above zero percent is breaking the law."*

His expression had held genuine regret, but that didn't soften the blow. Sympathy meant everything, even though the outcome didn't change. I had stood there, helpless, as Kathy was led away — her head held high, even with tears shining in her eyes. That image was burned into my memory; a reminder of just how fast life could derail.

As if he were standing in front of me, I could still picture his face clearly. The creases in his forehead, the way his eyes shifted like he wished the whole thing would just go away. However, duty has a way of silencing personal feelings. And that night, his duty was to enforce the law, no matter how much he seemed to hate it.

I remembered everything. The looks from the other passengers, eyes darting between us, faces wrapped in a blend of curiosity and judgment. I remembered the way Kathy glanced back at me right before the officer led her away. Her expression was torn between apology and regret. I remembered the hollow, sinking feeling in my chest as she turned and walked away.

My knuckles turned white as I tightened my grip on the steering wheel. No, I hadn't been able to stop what happened. But today, I would do everything in my power to help Kathy through this.

As the courthouse came into view, solid and imposing against the morning sky, I forced the doubts aside. The past was out of my hands. What mattered now was the present, and what I could do to make things right.

Entering the courthouse parking lot, the sight of the building's stark, austere facade hit me harder than I expected. This was where it would all be decided—not just for Kathy, but for both of us.

I pulled into a parking spot near the entrance, the crunch of gravel under the tires jarring against the quiet of the morning. I shut off the engine but didn't move. I just sat there, gripping the steering wheel, my palms damp and my pulse quickening. My heart pounded louder with each passing second, each beat a cruel countdown to whatever lay ahead.

Finally exhaling, I realized I'd been holding my breath. My hand found the door handle, and I stepped out of the car. The cool morning air hit me like a slap to the senses. In the distance, a bird chirped over and over, oblivious to the stress I was carrying.

I adjusted my shirt. The crisp white fabric felt stiff against my skin, unfamiliar. I'd picked this outfit carefully—the shirt and dark slacks I'd bought in town the day before. It wasn't much, but I hoped it said something. I wanted to look responsible and respectable. I wanted the judge—and anyone else watching—to see that we weren't reckless people. We didn't belong there. Not in this situation. Not in this place.

After locking the car, I started walking toward the entrance. With each step, a wave of determination surged through me. I couldn't control what the judge would decide, but I could control my support for Kathy, how I carried myself in this moment.

The courthouse stood ahead of me, silent and still. Its modest facade did little to reflect the gravity of what went on inside. Pale beige bricks and plain, square windows gave it the look of a government building trying hard not to be noticed—but to me, it loomed large and impersonal. Cold. Indifferent. A stark reminder that some things in life are simply beyond our control.

I quickly made my way up the steps, my mind racing with doubt. *Had we hired the right lawyer? Would the judge be able to see her for who she truly was—a woman of integrity who had made one mistake, not someone whose life deserved to be derailed?*

The thought of Kathy standing before a judge—vulnerable, exposed, her future resting in the hands of someone who didn't know her, didn't know us—made my stomach twist. Kathy was strong; I never doubted that, but this wasn't about strength. This was about standing in front of a system that only cared about facts, not the story behind them. It didn't matter how hard she'd worked, how much good she had done, or that this was a single irresponsible decision, not a pattern. To the judge, she'd be just another name on a docket. Another file. Another case to process before moving on.

The waiting was over. It was time to face the reality we'd been dreading. I drew in a long breath, trying to steady the slight tremor in my hands.

The helplessness I felt as it all unfolded in front of me will never be forgotten. It felt surreal—like something out of a movie. One of those over-the-top scenes people dismiss as exaggerated drama. I couldn't believe this was real. That this was happening to us.

When I finally reached the doors, I hesitated for just a moment. My hand rested on the cold metal handle as I braced myself for whatever was waiting inside. Whatever happened, I knew one thing with absolute certainty: I would stand by Kathy, no matter what.

With that resolve anchoring me, I pushed the door open and stepped inside, ready to face whatever decisions lay ahead for both of us.

Inside, the courthouse felt like a different world entirely—quiet, still, and unnaturally cool. The warmth of the sun I'd left behind felt like a distant memory. The faint murmur of voices drifted through the space, mingling with the soft shuffle of paperwork and the occasional ring of a desk phone echoing from an office down the hall. Every sound bounced slightly off the high ceilings, giving the place an eerie, almost reverent hush. I scanned the waiting area until my eyes found her.

Kathy was sitting near the far wall, framed by dull beige paint and the harsh glow of fluorescent lights. Even in those sterile surroundings, she stood out. Her presence had always had a kind of quiet strength, and now, more than ever, it was unmistakable. Her back was straight, maintaining good posture, and her hands were folded neatly in her lap. At a glance, she looked composed—graceful even—but I knew her too well.

The tension in her frame was evident, as was the slight stiffness in the way she sat. Her jaw was set just a little too firmly, her brow faintly furrowed. Her fingers were interlaced, gripped together a bit too tightly. She wasn't just sitting there—she was bracing herself. Steady on the outside, but battling a storm within.

Even in the middle of this crisis, she carried herself with dignity. Watching her in that moment made my heart ache—but it also made me proud. So damn proud.

My heart ached watching her like this. I hated seeing her like this—so vulnerable, even though she wore her strength like armor. Kathy had always been the one to face challenges head-on, her resilience shining through even in the darkest hours. But this... this wasn't like anything we'd ever faced before. This was the kind of trial that stripped you bare, exposing every fear and insecurity you thought you'd buried deep.

Yet, there she was—holding herself together with a quiet courage that only deepened my admiration for her.

My footsteps crossing the room were softened by the polished tile floor. Her eyes lifted as I approached, and for just a second, her mask slipped. I saw it—the worry she was working so hard to hide. But then she gave me a small, careful smile. It didn't quite reach her eyes, but it was enough. Enough to say I'm okay, even if she wasn't.

"You made it," she said softly. Her voice was steady but low, as if speaking too loudly might shatter the calm we were clinging to.

"Of course I did," I replied, giving her a long emotional hug. I sank into the seat beside her and reached for her hand. My own was warm and sure as it wrapped around hers. She tightened her grip, and for a long moment, we just sat like that—no words, no explanations. Just us. Just presence.

The quiet hum of the courthouse carried on around us—shuffling papers, murmured conversations, and distant footsteps. All of that faded to the background. Right then, there was only the weight of what we were about to face.

For a moment, we sat in silence, the weight of everything pressing down on us, somehow, it felt a little lighter just being together. I gently stroked the back of Kathy's hand with my thumb, a small, deliberate gesture to remind her she wasn't alone. All around us, the courthouse carried on—lawyers shuffling papers, clerks tapping away at keyboards, hushed voices trading legal jargon. To me, it all felt distant and unimportant. There was only us, holding on to each other in the face of what came next.

The quiet was broken by the arrival of our lawyer, Mr. Garrison. He approached with a composed demeanor, and every detail about him was meticulous. The dark, well-tailored suit, polished shoes, and a leather briefcase held tightly in one hand. He didn't say much, but you could feel the steadiness in every step he took. When he reached us, he gave a polite nod before speaking.

"It's a straightforward case," he said, his voice calm and professional. "Kathy, your decision to plead guilty will likely result in a lenient sentence. The judge will appreciate your honesty. Just remain respectful, and answer his questions directly and truthfully."

Kathy nodded, and I watched a little of the tension leave her face. Something about Mr. Garrison's quiet confidence gave us a little more footing, as if his steadiness could carry some of the burden for us.

"Yes, I understand," she said, her voice soft but steady.

Leaning in so our shoulders touched, I gave her hand another squeeze. I whispered, just for her to hear. "You've got this."

She turned and gave me the faintest smile—fragile, but real. In that moment, I was reminded again just how strong she really was.

Mr. Garrison glanced at his watch, then nodded toward the doors leading into the courtroom. "It's time," he said simply.

Kathy's hand was tense in mine, and I gave it one last squeeze before slowly letting go. She stood carefully, smoothing the front of her blouse with hands that trembled just slightly. Then, without a word, we followed Mr. Garrison toward the courtroom doors.

The hearing was brief, but to me, it felt like time had slowed to a crawl. I sat in the back row of the courtroom, gripping the edge of the wooden bench.

Kathy stood at the front, facing the judge. Her posture was upright, but I could see the slight tremble in her hands as they rested by her sides. When the judge finally spoke, his voice boomed through the room—deep, commanding, every word landing with weight.

"Mrs. Erck, you are charged with possession and smuggling of marijuana. Do you understand the charges against you, and how do you plead?" he said with a plain expression across his face.

Kathy took a breath, steadying herself.

"Yes, Your Honor," she said, her voice calm but firm as she entered her plea. "Guilty."

She owned her mistake without shrinking from it. Her words were measured, deliberate, and sincere. No deflection. No excuses. Just honesty—raw and quiet. As I listened, pride and heartache twisted together in my heart.

I knew how much courage it took for her to stand there and speak with such honesty—to own her mistake so openly, knowing the courtroom was listening, judging. The judge remained silent, his face illegible, but I caught something—a small shift in his expression. The faintest softening around the edges. It wasn't much, but it was enough to let in a sliver of hope.

When Kathy finished speaking, the room went still. A heavy silence settled over everything. The judge leaned back in his chair, studying her as he deliberated. The pause stretched endlessly. I could hear the tick of the courtroom clock, each second like a drumbeat. I held my breath, heart pounding, waiting for him to speak.

Finally, he leaned forward, hands resting flat on the desk.

"Mrs. Erck," he began, his voice even but firm. "Your honesty and acceptance of responsibility are commendable. However, the court must still impose a penalty for your actions."

My stomach dropped. Every word that followed landed like a rock.

The judge spoke, his tone firm but not unkind, "I'm sentencing you to six months of probation—but that sentence will be suspended. You are also ordered to pay a fine of $1,500 plus court fees. You are free to return home to New Jersey. Just stay out of trouble because this is on your record going forward."

A deep breath escaped, and so did the tension that had built up in me for the past few days. It wasn't a perfect outcome—we both knew that—but it was so much better than the scenarios I'd played out in my head during all those sleepless nights. The worst-case endings, the irreversible consequences. Now, standing there in that courtroom, I felt something unfamiliar creeping in—relief like the first bit of sunlight peeking through storm clouds.

At the front of the room, Kathy stood still for a moment, the echo of the judge's gavel hanging in the air. It felt final, like a closing chapter. I watched as she slowly turned from the podium.

There was so much written on her face: relief, gratitude, and just a flicker of vulnerability that she rarely let anyone see. It was like she was saying *thank you for being here. Thank you for believing in me.* I felt it as clearly as if the words had been spoken aloud.

Immediately, I gave her the faintest nod in return. *Always*, I thought.

In that quiet exchange, we didn't need words. I'd always admired the grace with which she carried herself through even the hardest moments. I also saw the toll it took. The exhaustion in her expression, the trace of fear that still lingered despite the relief. Kathy was strong—undeniably, but she wasn't unbreakable. Her humanity made her sensitivity even more beautiful to me. It was her ability to endure while still feeling the pain that made me love her even more.

She walked toward me slowly, each step sure, her chin held high despite the humility I knew she was carrying. When she finally reached me, she paused. Her lips parted like she wanted to say something, but no words came out. She didn't need to say anything. I reached out my hand, and she took it without hesitation. A gesture that said everything that didn't need to be spoken.

The sunlight poured across the marble steps, casting a golden glow that seemed almost too soft for what we'd just been through. The light bounced off nearby windows, bright and warm, as if the world—unaware of the storm we'd weathered—was offering a kind of quiet mercy. Cars rolled past, horns blared in the distance, and people on the sidewalks chatted. It all felt strangely surreal, this routine life continuing around us, even as we stood there changed by the recent events.

Kathy stood beside me on the courthouse steps, her gaze locked on the street below. She wasn't watching anything specific;

she was just taking in the motion, the noise, and the life. I think it reminded her that the world hadn't stopped while she was locked up.

The breeze caught a few strands of her hair and swept them gently across her face. She didn't move to fix them. Instead, a smile broke out and turned her face into a happy relief.

She turned her head slightly, acknowledging me with a soft, almost wistful smile. Her voice was barely a whisper, but it carried the full weight of everything she'd been holding in.

Her words cut straight to my heart. "I'm sorry you had to go through this," she said, her words laced with both regret and gratitude.

Immediately, I shook my head, meeting her gaze with a steady, reassuring look. "No apologies, Kath," I said gently. "What matters is we're moving forward. This isn't the end—just a bump in the road."

Her eyes shimmered as she turned fully to face me. The smile she gave me was small but sure, though I could see the vulnerability behind it—the kind she only ever let me see.

Her voice catching just slightly, "I don't know how I would've done this without you," she said.

"You'll never have to find out," I told her, my voice quiet but certain.

Letting the promise sink in, I held her gaze, not just in words, but in presence, in the way I stood beside her. It wasn't just reassurance. It was a vow.

For a moment, we stood there together on the courthouse steps, the noise of the world around us fading into nothing. I reached for her hand, and she met me halfway, in a gesture so simple, yet so full of meaning. In that touch was everything we'd been through—the fear, the strength, the unspoken vow that we were still standing.

As we started walking toward the car, Kathy's steps grew lighter, as if the burden she'd been carrying had finally loosened its grip. Her shoulders eased, and the tightness in her hand softened. She wasn't clinging now; she was back to normal, my wife, Kathy, present and confident.

The walk to the car wasn't long, but it felt meaningful. A quiet procession away from everything that had just happened, and toward whatever was next. For the first time in what felt like forever, I let myself believe—we will be okay.

We didn't talk. We didn't need to. The silence between us was full—full of understanding and reassurance.

When we reached the car, I opened the door for her. She looked up at me and smiled—a real smile, open and unguarded. The kind of smile that reminded me of everything I loved about her.

In that moment, my heart felt lighter than it had in days, and I smiled back.

# Chapter 15
# A Story for the Ages

The flight home was quiet. Kathy rested her head against my shoulder, her fingers loosely laced with mine as we stared out at the endless sky before us. The low hum of the plane, the occasional turn of a page from someone a few rows back, the soft murmur of voices—it all faded into the background.

We had made it not just through the wedding, but through unforeseen trials that had tested us in ways we never could've predicted.

Slowly, I let out a breath I had been holding and shifted in my seat, glancing down at Kathy. "So… I guess we're officially married," I murmured, a small smile tugging at the corner of my mouth.

Kathy chuckled, her eyes still fixed on the clouds outside the window. "You sure? Because without that marriage license in hand, technically, we could've just been two fools on a costly, ridiculous vacation."

Sighing and full of mock drama, I added, "If we don't get that thing in the mail, I'm demanding a redo. Preferably somewhere without brothels this time."

She nudged me with her elbow, smiling. "No promises."

As the plane began its descent, the feeling of home came rushing back—not just in the familiar landscape unfolding below us, but something more profound. That quiet recognition that no matter how far we'd traveled, this was where real life was waiting to begin. The tropical sun was behind us now, replaced by the crisp bite of autumn air. As we stepped off the plane, the scent of damp leaves and chimney smoke wrapped around us like a welcome back. It was the season of change, and somehow, that felt exactly right.

The changes in us had been monumental. The exhaustion we currently felt was overwhelmed with contentment and a satisfying feeling that we were finally home. Instead of returning refreshed, glowing, and blissfully relaxed, we came back battle-tested and jet-lagged, carrying not just souvenirs, but stories, ones we knew we'd be telling for the rest of our lives.

Gently, I closed my leather journal and placed it on the mantel, knowing I would be sharing the stories again.

\*\*\*

Six months later, the day arrived for our long-awaited family wedding party. Months of planning had gone into it, and when we first imagined this moment, we never would have thought of the amazing tale we would have to share with our family at this party.

The moment we stepped through the front door, the room exploded with cheers, hugs, and the clink of raised glasses. Friends and family surrounded us, showering us with congratulations and a thousand questions, everyone eager to hear how our honeymoon had gone.

Margaret, Kathy's sister, narrowed her eyes almost immediately. "Alright, spill. You two look way too smug for this to have been an uneventful honeymoon."

Kathy glanced at me, and we shared a look—one of those silent exchanges that held a whole story in it. Then she turned to Margaret, a slow, knowing smile spreading across her face as she picked up a glass of wine from the table.

"Oh, Margaret," she said with a grin. "You have no idea."

The wedding party was exactly how we'd imagined it. Our home buzzed with conversation, the clinking of glasses, and laughter drifting in from every corner. The dining table was piled with trays of food, each one arranged with the kind of precision only my mother could demand. Meanwhile, a small cluster of cousins hovered near the bar, already placing bets on who could down the most champagne without Aunt Louise catching them in the act.

Kathy moved gracefully through the room, greeting everyone with smiles and hugs. I could see the way it was hitting her—this surreal shift from the chaos we'd just lived through to the warmth and comfort of being home. We'd been through a lot—married, stranded, lost, arrested, and somehow, through it all, we'd found even more reasons to love each other. Now, in the middle of this celebration, she finally looked like she could breathe again.

As for me? I was in full storytelling mode.

I'd been pulled into a circle, everyone leaning in, eyes wide, waiting to hear what kind of disaster we'd narrowly survived. I was happy to deliver.

"So there we are," I said, arms flying as I set the scene, "standing in the middle of a deserted airport, completely stranded. No phones, no ship, no clue what to do. Kathy—cool as ever—just looks at me and goes, 'Well, this is romantic.'"

Margaret gasped. "Wait, wait, wait—you lost the actual cruise ship?"

"Oh, not just lost it," I said, laying it on thick. "We watched it sail away in real time."

The room exploded with laughter and disbelief mixed with pure delight.

Kathy leaned back against the counter, shaking her head. "And do you know what this genius does? He pays two hundred bucks to use a payphone. A payphone! Just to call the cruise line and beg them to turn the WindStar around."

Holding up one finger, I indicated, "It was a logical plan."

"No, Bob," she said with that signature smirk. "It was desperation."

More laughter followed, and I raised both hands in mock surrender. "Alright, fine. Guilty. Let's not forget who found the only available hotel room that night."

The room quieted just enough for the punchline to land.

Greg squinted. "Wait… this isn't the part where you guys…?"

Kathy let out a sigh. "Yes, Greg. We slept in a brothel."

That was it. The room erupted again.

Grinning as the laughter echoed around us. "And that, folks, is the story of how we started our marriage in the single most questionable hotel in all of Tahiti."

Margaret wiped tears from her eyes. "Oh my god, this is gold."

Kathy chuckled, taking a sip of her drink. "Well, just when we thought that was the last of it, we got one final surprise."

She reached into a drawer and pulled out a folded newspaper.

"This," she said, tapping it, "is how the Hawaiian court decided to return my passport and marriage license."

Letting out a sigh. I shook my head, "Months later. Wrapped in cartoons."

Greg nearly fell out of his chair. "You're kidding."

Kathy reached into the folder and unfolded the paper, revealing the absurd comic strips wrapped around the official documents. "I wish we were."

The whole room erupted again, laughter spilling into every corner. I took a long sip of my drink, smiling as I glanced around at the people we loved, then sighed with a kind of amused surrender.

"And that," I said, shaking my head, "was the moment I realized our life together would always be filled with hills and valleys, joys and sorrows, and oh, so much mystery!"

Kathy grinned and looked at me. "And honestly? I wouldn't have it any other way."

*Thanksgiving: Where the Story Lives Forever*

# THE END

Made in the USA
Columbia, SC
28 January 2026

60c336e5-a1e8-45d2-8d80-a02a40f73a87R01